DEC 1 3 2013

GREEN LANTERN

THE ANIMATED SERIES ™

STONE ARCH BOOKS
a capstone imprint

STONE ARCH BOOKS™
Published in 2013
A Capstone Imprint
1710 Roe Crest Drive
North Mankato, MN 56003
www.capstonepub.com

DC Comics
1700 Broadway, New York, NY 10019
A Warner Bros. Entertainment Company

Cataloging-in-Publication Data is available at the Library of Congress website:
ISBN: 978-1-4342-4796-4 (library binding)

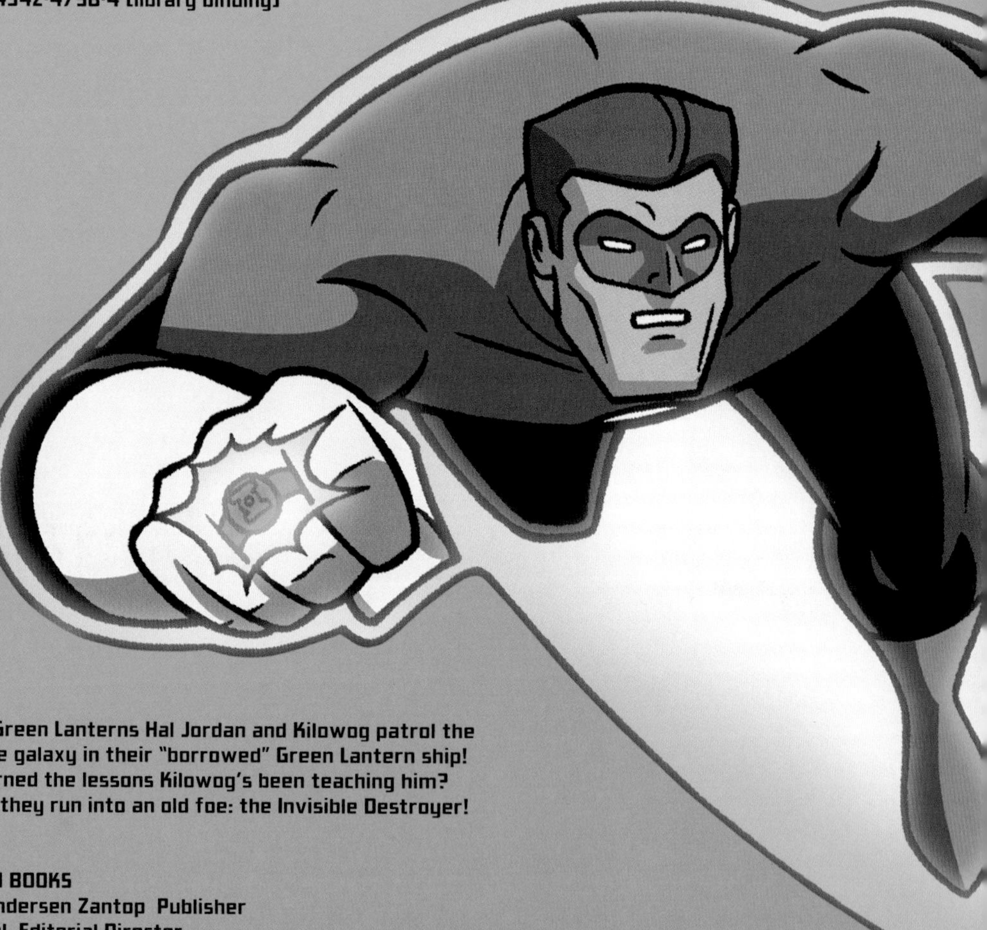

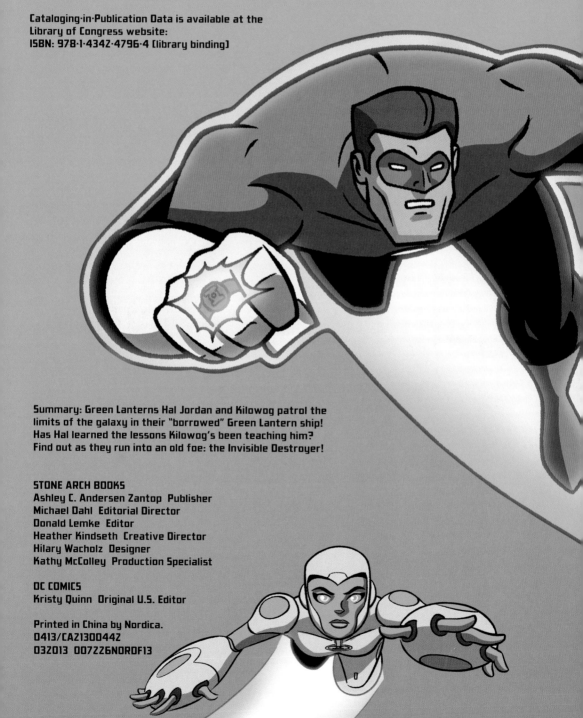

Summary: Green Lanterns Hal Jordan and Kilowog patrol the limits of the galaxy in their "borrowed" Green Lantern ship! Has Hal learned the lessons Kilowog's been teaching him? Find out as they run into an old foe: the Invisible Destroyer!

STONE ARCH BOOKS
Ashley C. Andersen Zantop Publisher
Michael Dahl Editorial Director
Donald Lemke Editor
Heather Kindseth Creative Director
Hilary Wacholz Designer
Kathy McColley Production Specialist

DC COMICS
Kristy Quinn Original U.S. Editor

Printed in China by Nordica.
0413/CA21300442
032013 007226NORDF13

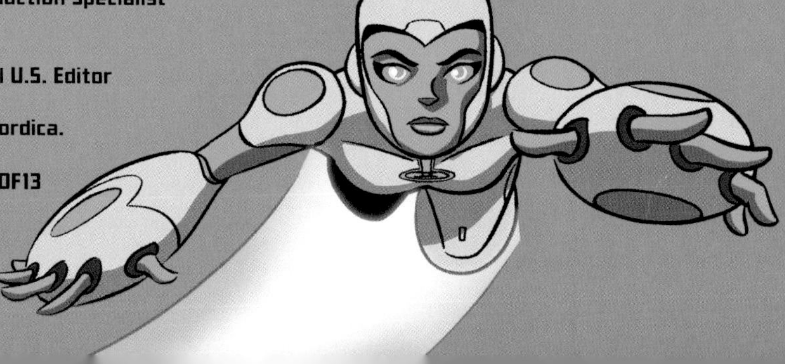

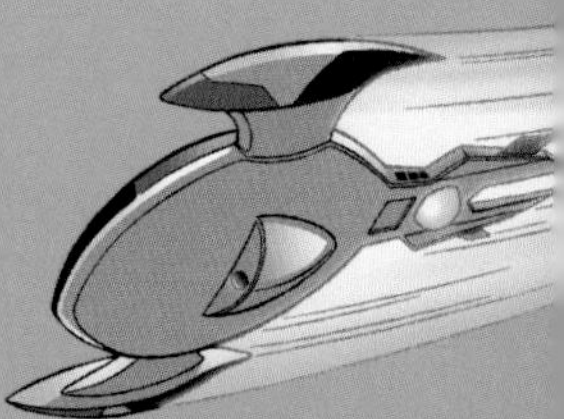

GREEN LANTERN

THE ANIMATED SERIES™

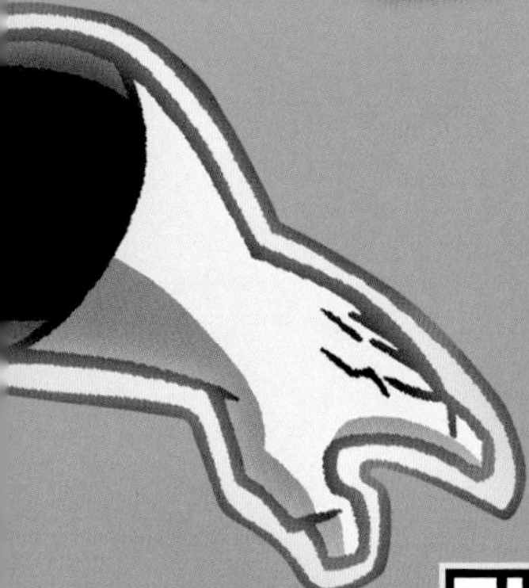

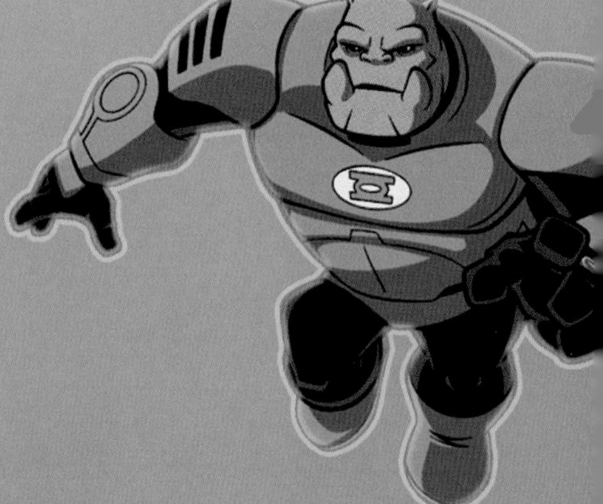

THE INVISIBLE DESTROYER

Art Baltazar & Franco....................writers
Dario Brizuela............................ illustrator
Gabe Eltaeb & Dario Brizuela.....colorists
Saida Abbott ....letterer

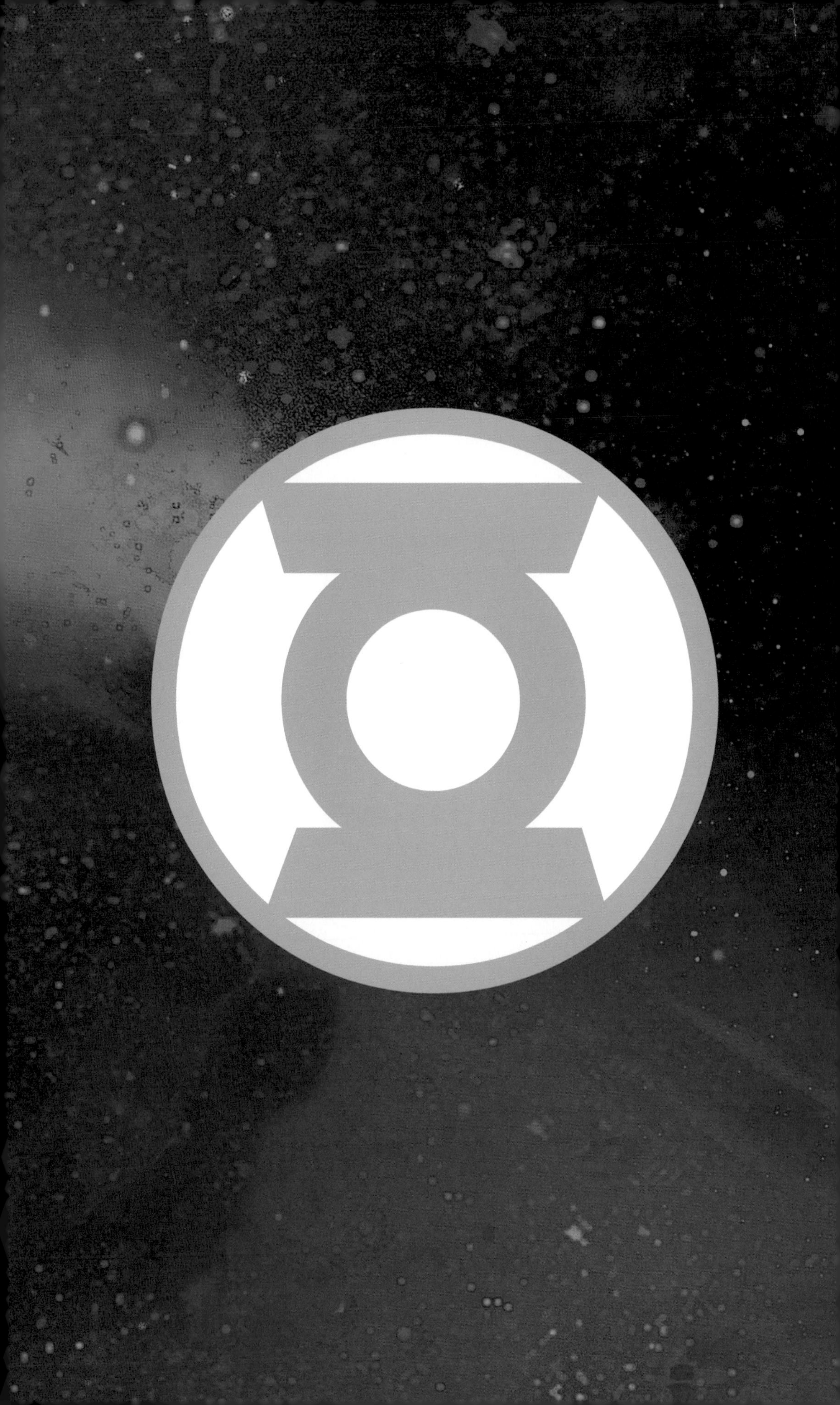

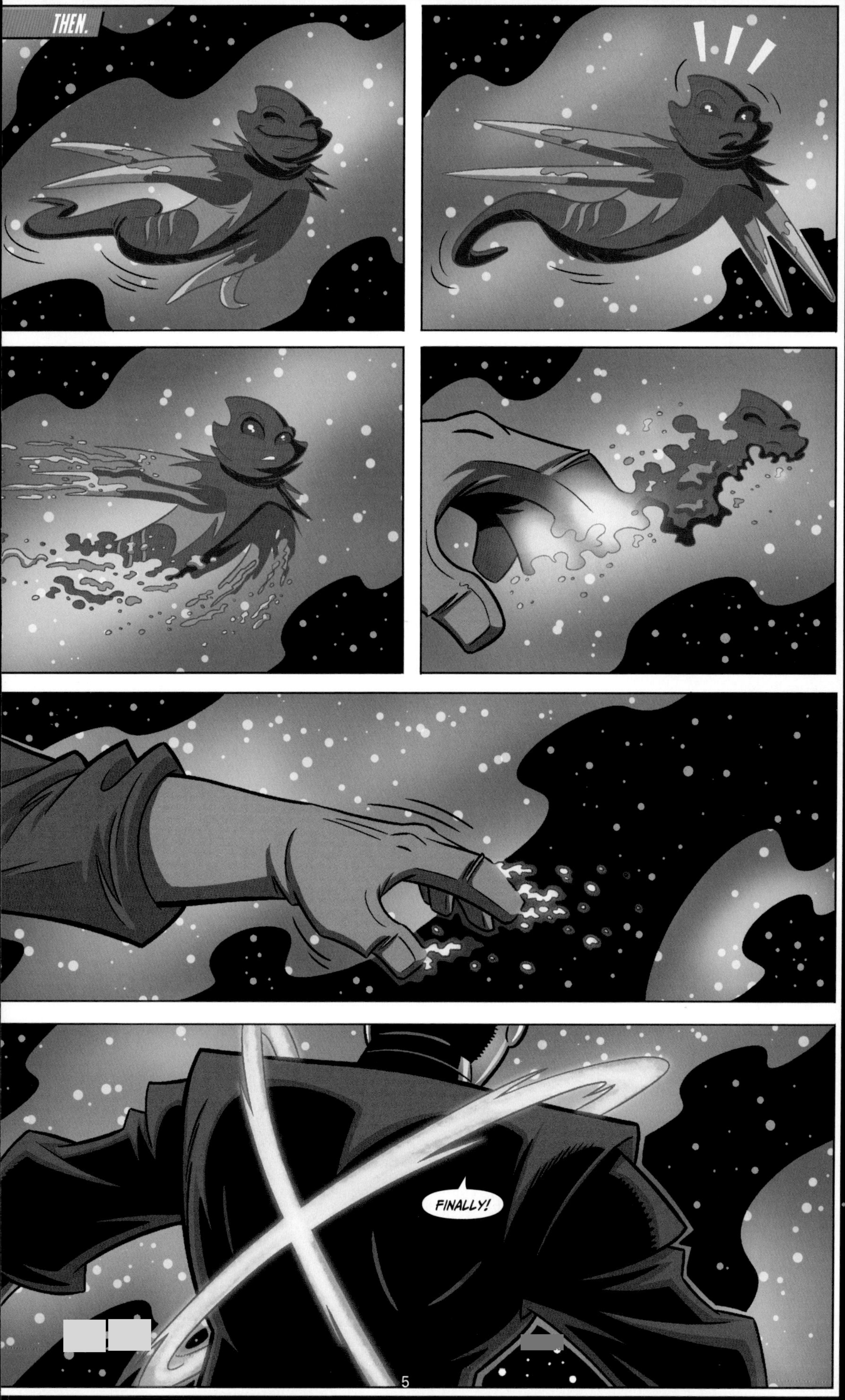
THEN.
FINALLY!

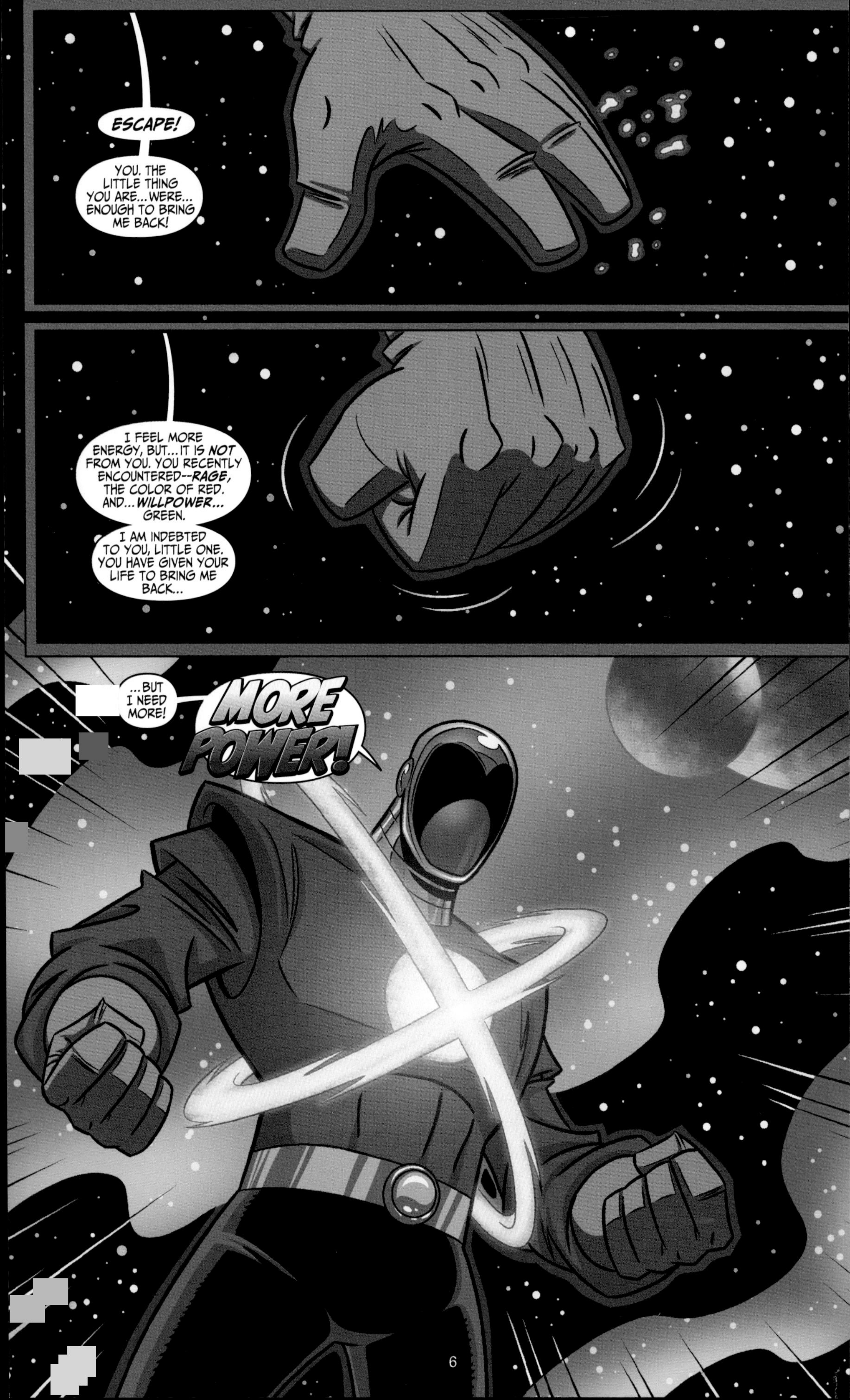

ESCAPE!
YOU. THE LITTLE THING YOU ARE... WERE... ENOUGH TO BRING ME BACK!
I FEEL MORE ENERGY, BUT... IT IS NOT FROM YOU. YOU RECENTLY ENCOUNTERED--RAGE, THE COLOR OF RED. AND... WILLPOWER... GREEN.
I AM INDEBTED TO YOU, LITTLE ONE. YOU HAVE GIVEN YOUR LIFE TO BRING ME BACK...
...BUT I NEED MORE!
MORE POWER!

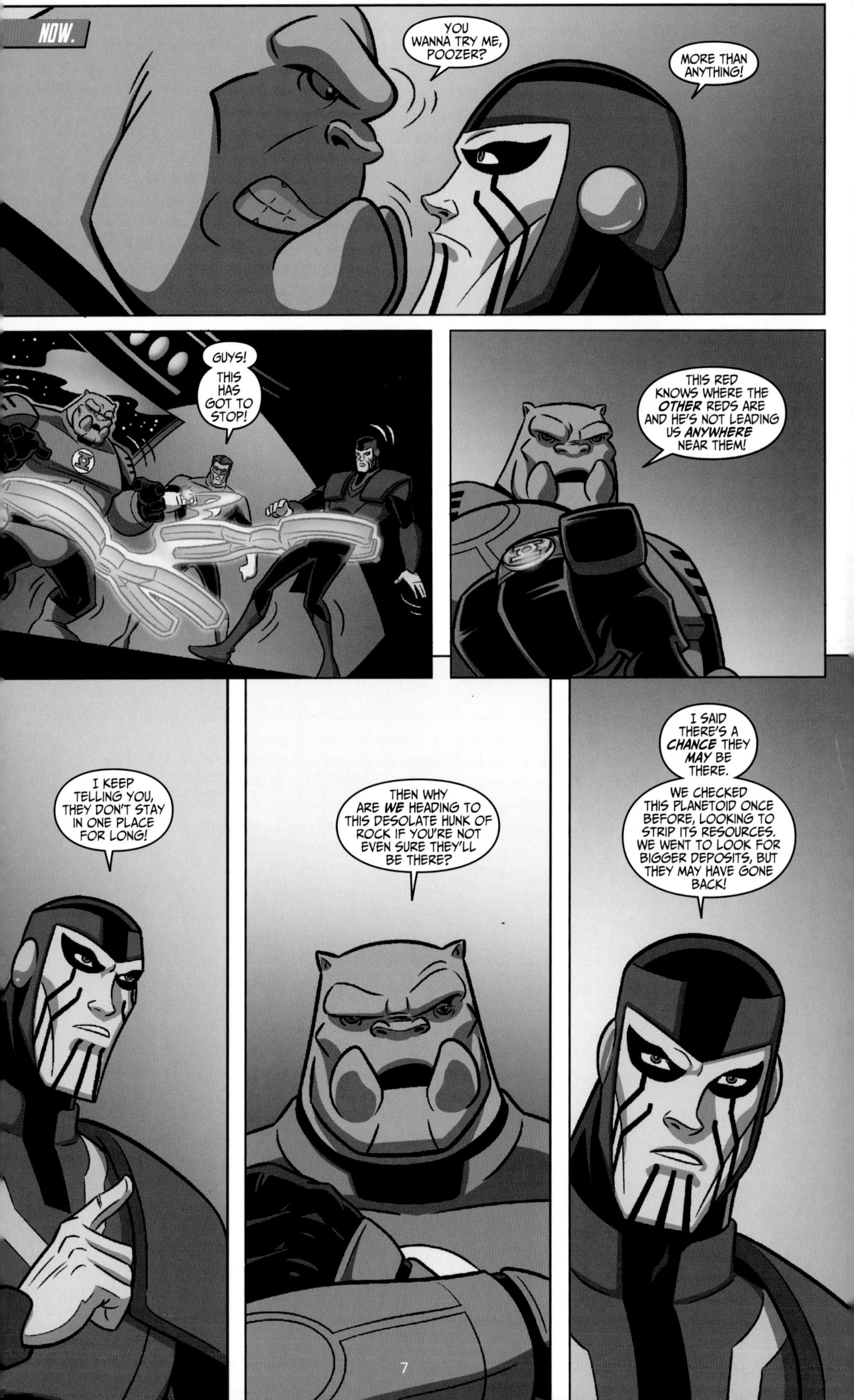

NOW.
YOU WANNA TRY ME, POOZER?
MORE THAN ANYTHING!
GUYS! THIS HAS GOT TO STOP!
THIS RED KNOWS WHERE THE *OTHER* REDS ARE AND HE'S NOT LEADING US *ANYWHERE* NEAR THEM!
I KEEP TELLING YOU, THEY DON'T STAY IN ONE PLACE FOR LONG!
THEN WHY ARE *WE* HEADING TO THIS DESOLATE HUNK OF ROCK IF YOU'RE NOT EVEN SURE THEY'LL BE THERE?
I SAID THERE'S A *CHANCE* THEY *MAY* BE THERE.
WE CHECKED THIS PLANETOID ONCE BEFORE, LOOKING TO STRIP ITS RESOURCES. WE WENT TO LOOK FOR BIGGER DEPOSITS, BUT THEY MAY HAVE GONE BACK!

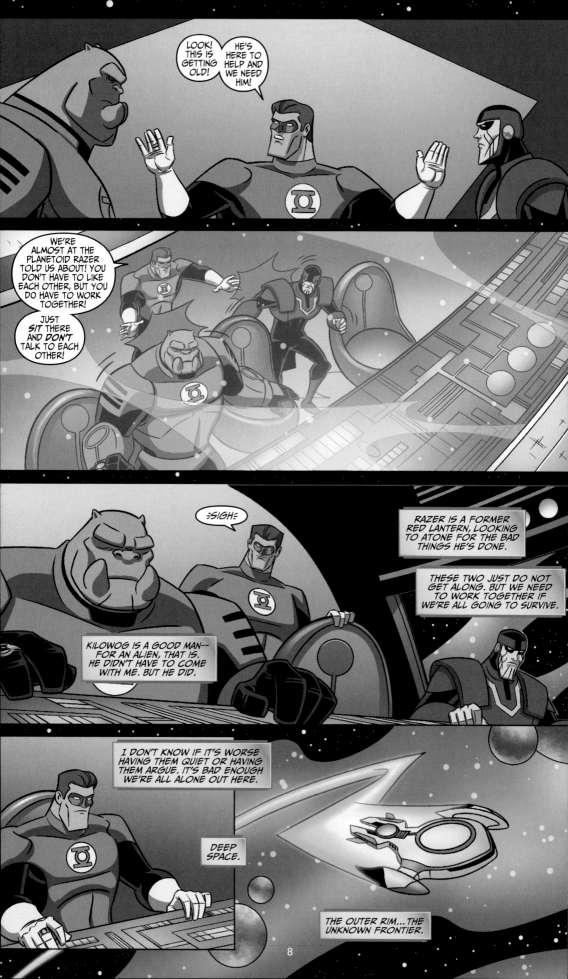

LOOK! THIS IS GETTING OLD!

HE'S HERE TO HELP AND WE NEED HIM!

WE'RE ALMOST AT THE PLANETOID RAZER TOLD US ABOUT! YOU DON'T HAVE TO LIKE EACH OTHER, BUT YOU DO HAVE TO WORK TOGETHER!

JUST *SIT* THERE AND *DON'T* TALK TO EACH OTHER!

≡SIGH≡

RAZER IS A FORMER RED LANTERN, LOOKING TO ATONE FOR THE BAD THINGS HE'S DONE.

THESE TWO JUST DO NOT GET ALONG. BUT WE NEED TO WORK TOGETHER IF WE'RE ALL GOING TO SURVIVE.

KILOWOG IS A GOOD MAN-- FOR AN ALIEN, THAT IS. HE DIDN'T HAVE TO COME WITH ME. BUT HE DID.

I DON'T KNOW IF IT'S WORSE HAVING THEM QUIET OR HAVING THEM ARGUE. IT'S BAD ENOUGH WE'RE ALL ALONE OUT HERE.

DEEP SPACE.

THE OUTER RIM...THE UNKNOWN FRONTIER.

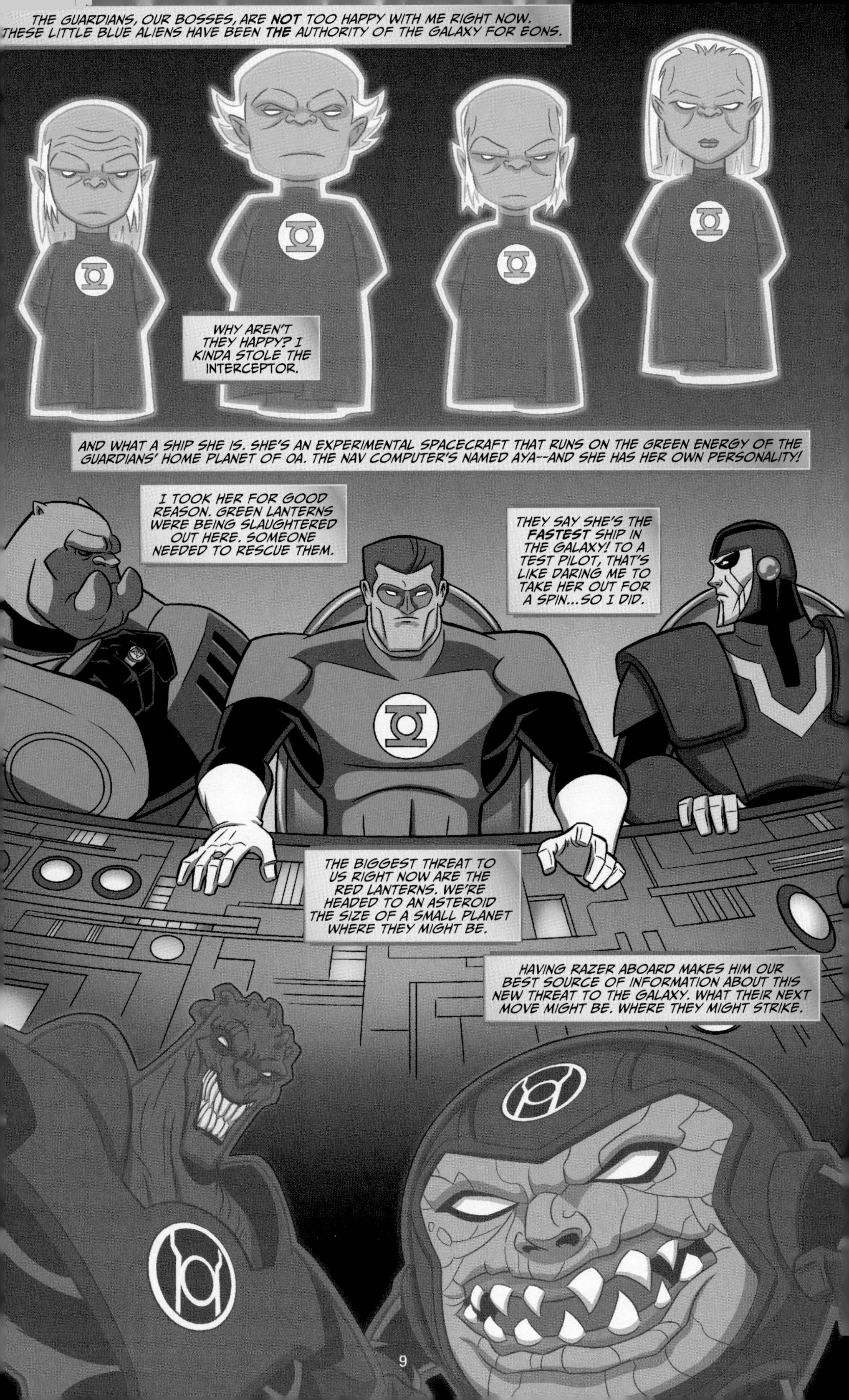
THE GUARDIANS, OUR BOSSES, ARE NOT TOO HAPPY WITH ME RIGHT NOW. THESE LITTLE BLUE ALIENS HAVE BEEN THE AUTHORITY OF THE GALAXY FOR EONS.
WHY AREN'T THEY HAPPY? I KINDA STOLE THE INTERCEPTOR.
AND WHAT A SHIP SHE IS. SHE'S AN EXPERIMENTAL SPACECRAFT THAT RUNS ON THE GREEN ENERGY OF THE GUARDIANS' HOME PLANET OF OA. THE NAV COMPUTER'S NAMED AYA--AND SHE HAS HER OWN PERSONALITY!
I TOOK HER FOR GOOD REASON. GREEN LANTERNS WERE BEING SLAUGHTERED OUT HERE. SOMEONE NEEDED TO RESCUE THEM.
THEY SAY SHE'S THE FASTEST SHIP IN THE GALAXY! TO A TEST PILOT, THAT'S LIKE DARING ME TO TAKE HER OUT FOR A SPIN...SO I DID.
THE BIGGEST THREAT TO US RIGHT NOW ARE THE RED LANTERNS. WE'RE HEADED TO AN ASTEROID THE SIZE OF A SMALL PLANET WHERE THEY MIGHT BE.
HAVING RAZER ABOARD MAKES HIM OUR BEST SOURCE OF INFORMATION ABOUT THIS NEW THREAT TO THE GALAXY. WHAT THEIR NEXT MOVE MIGHT BE. WHERE THEY MIGHT STRIKE.

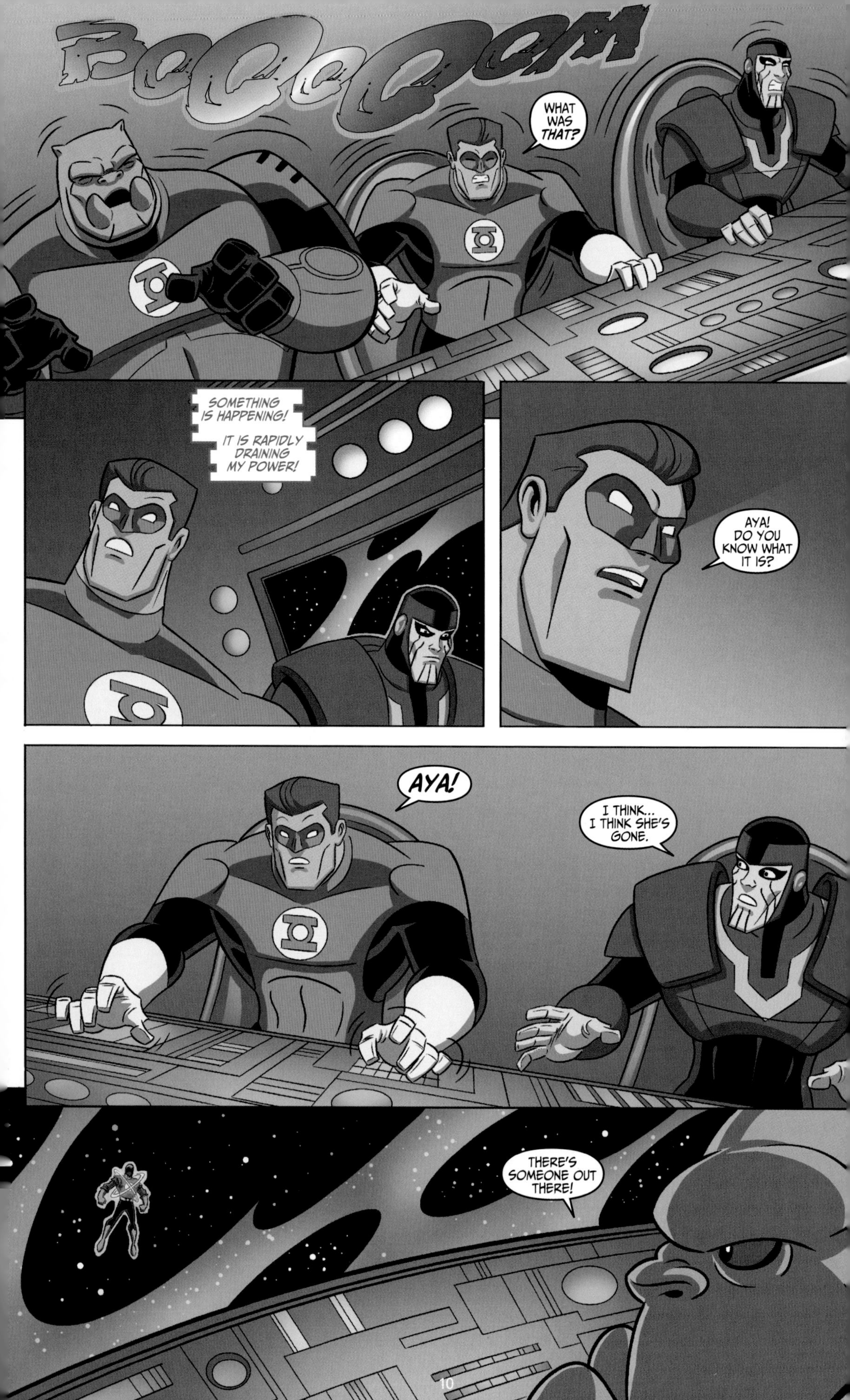
BOOOOOOM
WHAT WAS THAT?
SOMETHING IS HAPPENING!
IT IS RAPIDLY DRAINING MY POWER!
AYA! DO YOU KNOW WHAT IT IS?
AYA!
I THINK... I THINK SHE'S GONE.
THERE'S SOMEONE OUT THERE!

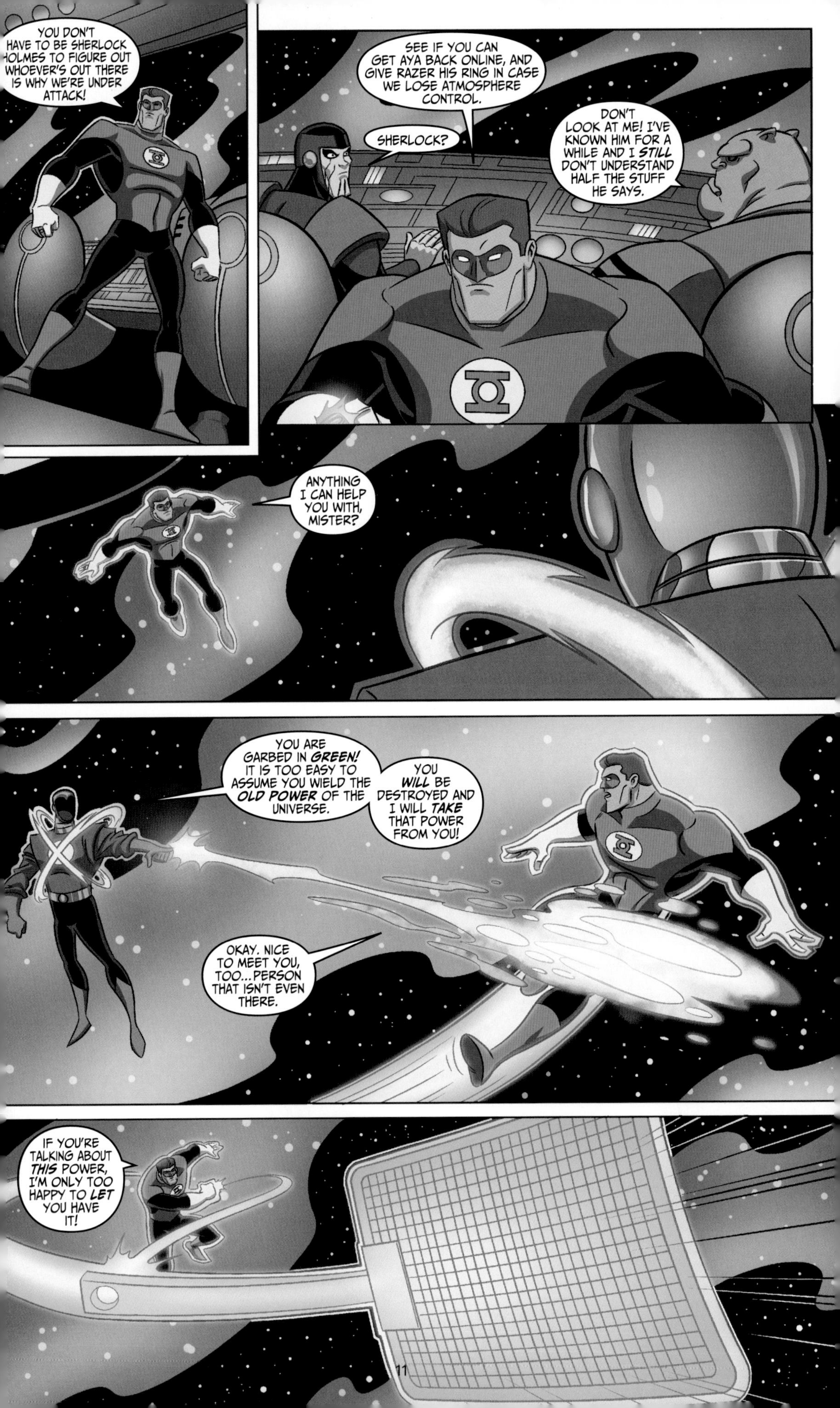
YOU DON'T HAVE TO BE SHERLOCK HOLMES TO FIGURE OUT WHOEVER'S OUT THERE IS WHY WE'RE UNDER ATTACK!
SEE IF YOU CAN GET AYA BACK ONLINE, AND GIVE RAZER HIS RING IN CASE WE LOSE ATMOSPHERE CONTROL.
SHERLOCK?
DON'T LOOK AT ME! I'VE KNOWN HIM FOR A WHILE AND I STILL DON'T UNDERSTAND HALF THE STUFF HE SAYS.
ANYTHING I CAN HELP YOU WITH, MISTER?
YOU ARE GARBED IN GREEN! IT IS TOO EASY TO ASSUME YOU WIELD THE OLD POWER OF THE UNIVERSE.
YOU WILL BE DESTROYED AND I WILL TAKE THAT POWER FROM YOU!
OKAY. NICE TO MEET YOU, TOO...PERSON THAT ISN'T EVEN THERE.
IF YOU'RE TALKING ABOUT THIS POWER, I'M ONLY TOO HAPPY TO LET YOU HAVE IT!

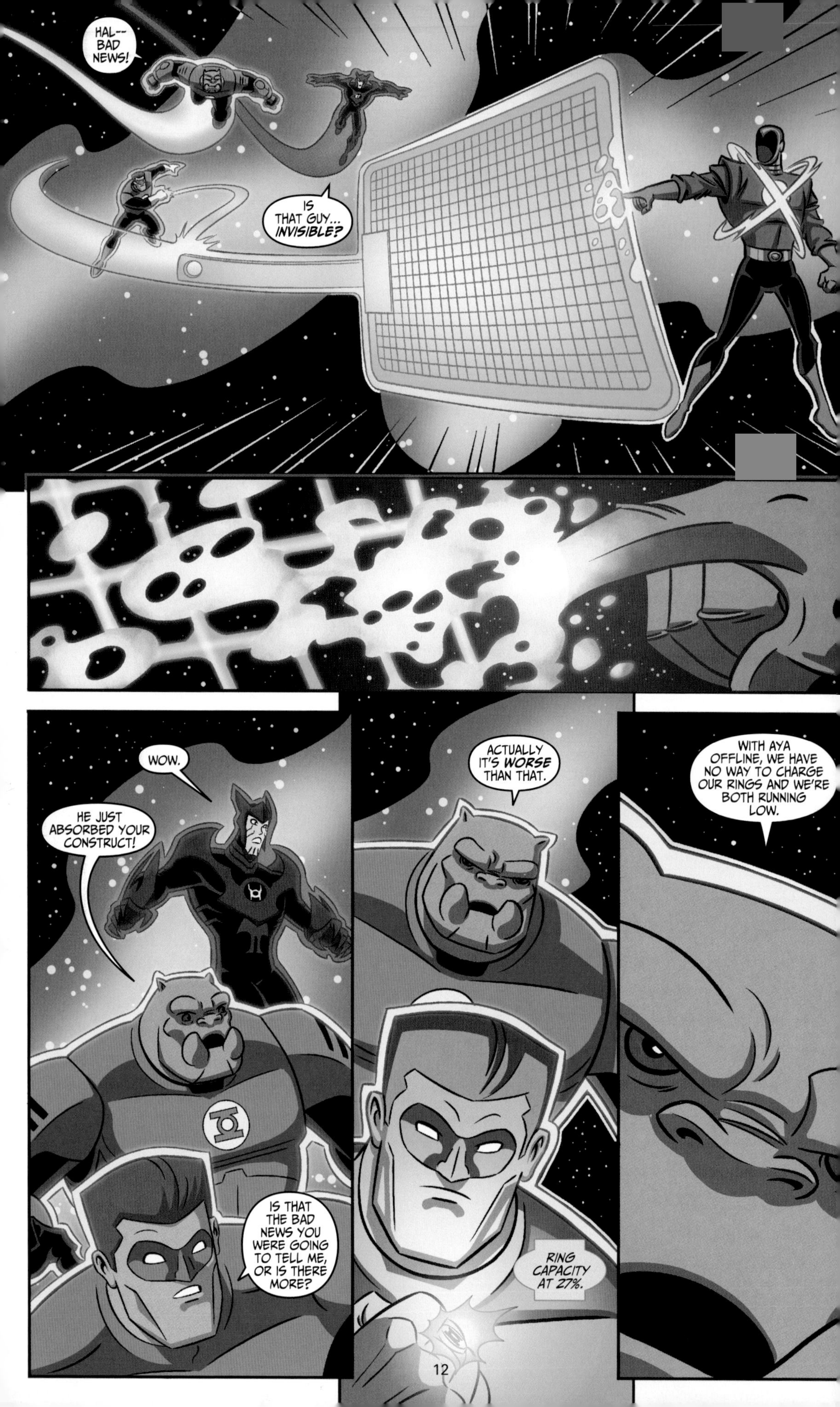

HAL--
BAD
NEWS!
IS
THAT GUY...
INVISIBLE?
WOW.
HE JUST
ABSORBED YOUR
CONSTRUCT!
IS THAT
THE BAD
NEWS YOU
WERE GOING
TO TELL ME,
OR IS THERE
MORE?
ACTUALLY
IT'S WORSE
THAN THAT.
RING
CAPACITY
AT 27%.
WITH AYA
OFFLINE, WE HAVE
NO WAY TO CHARGE
OUR RINGS AND WE'RE
BOTH RUNNING
LOW.

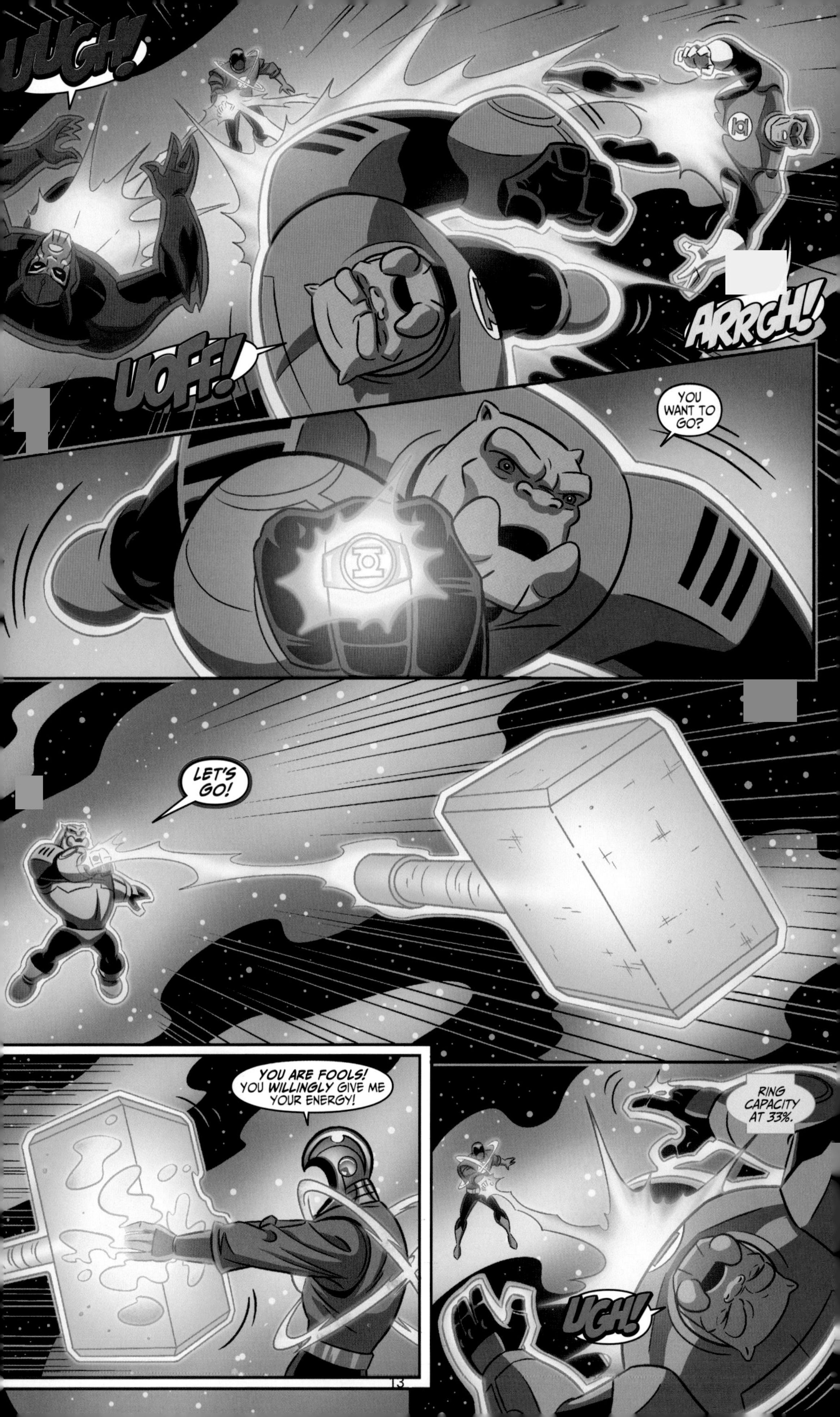
UUGH!
UOFF!
ARRGH!
YOU WANT TO GO?
LET'S GO!
YOU ARE FOOLS! YOU WILLINGLY GIVE ME YOUR ENERGY!
RING CAPACITY AT 33%.
UGH!

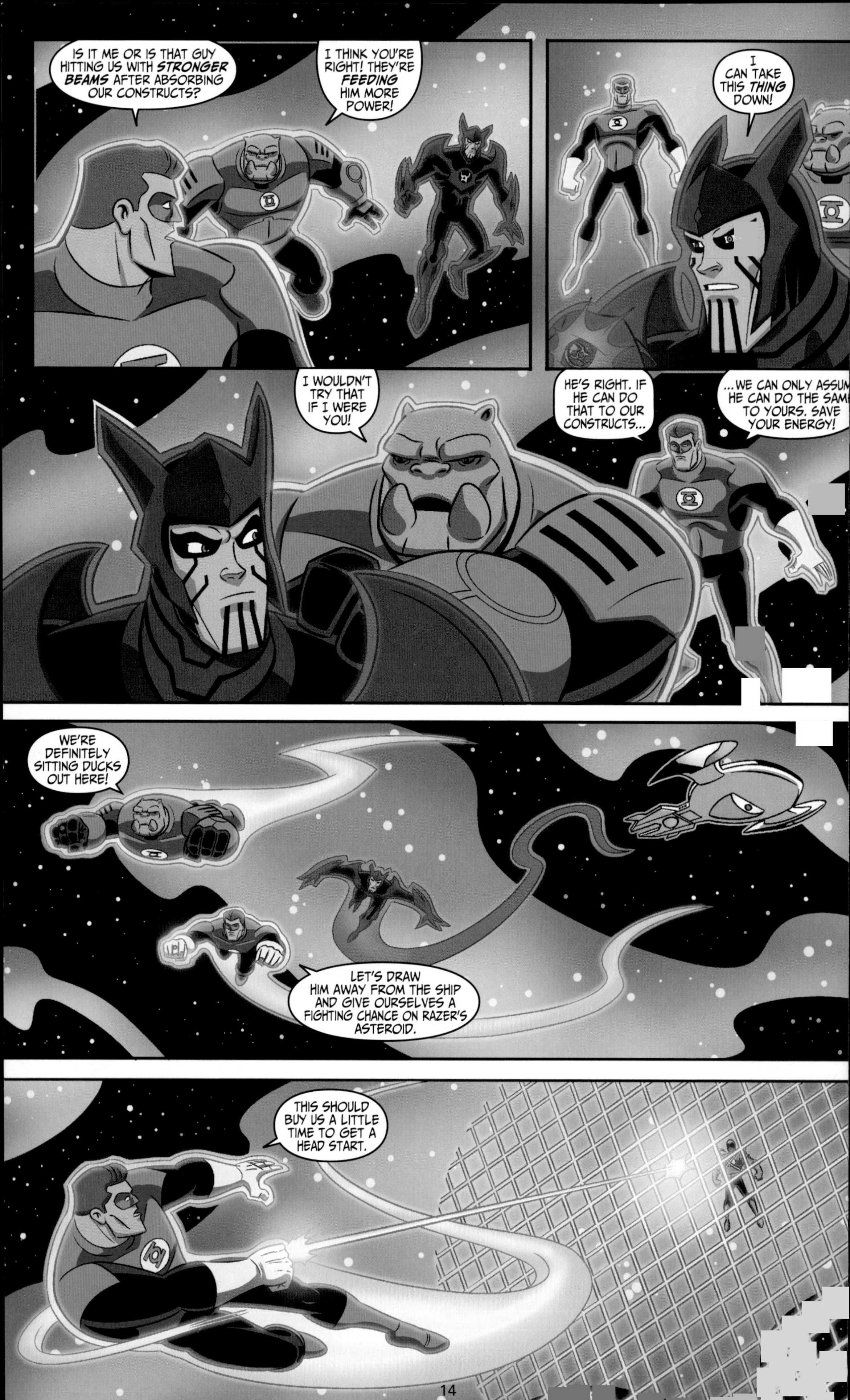

IS IT ME OR IS THAT GUY HITTING US WITH STRONGER BEAMS AFTER ABSORBING OUR CONSTRUCTS?
I THINK YOU'RE RIGHT! THEY'RE FEEDING HIM MORE POWER!
I CAN TAKE THIS THING DOWN!
I WOULDN'T TRY THAT IF I WERE YOU!
HE'S RIGHT. IF HE CAN DO THAT TO OUR CONSTRUCTS...
...WE CAN ONLY ASSUM HE CAN DO THE SAM TO YOURS. SAVE YOUR ENERGY!
WE'RE DEFINITELY SITTING DUCKS OUT HERE!
LET'S DRAW HIM AWAY FROM THE SHIP AND GIVE OURSELVES A FIGHTING CHANCE ON RAZER'S ASTEROID.
THIS SHOULD BUY US A LITTLE TIME TO GET A HEAD START.

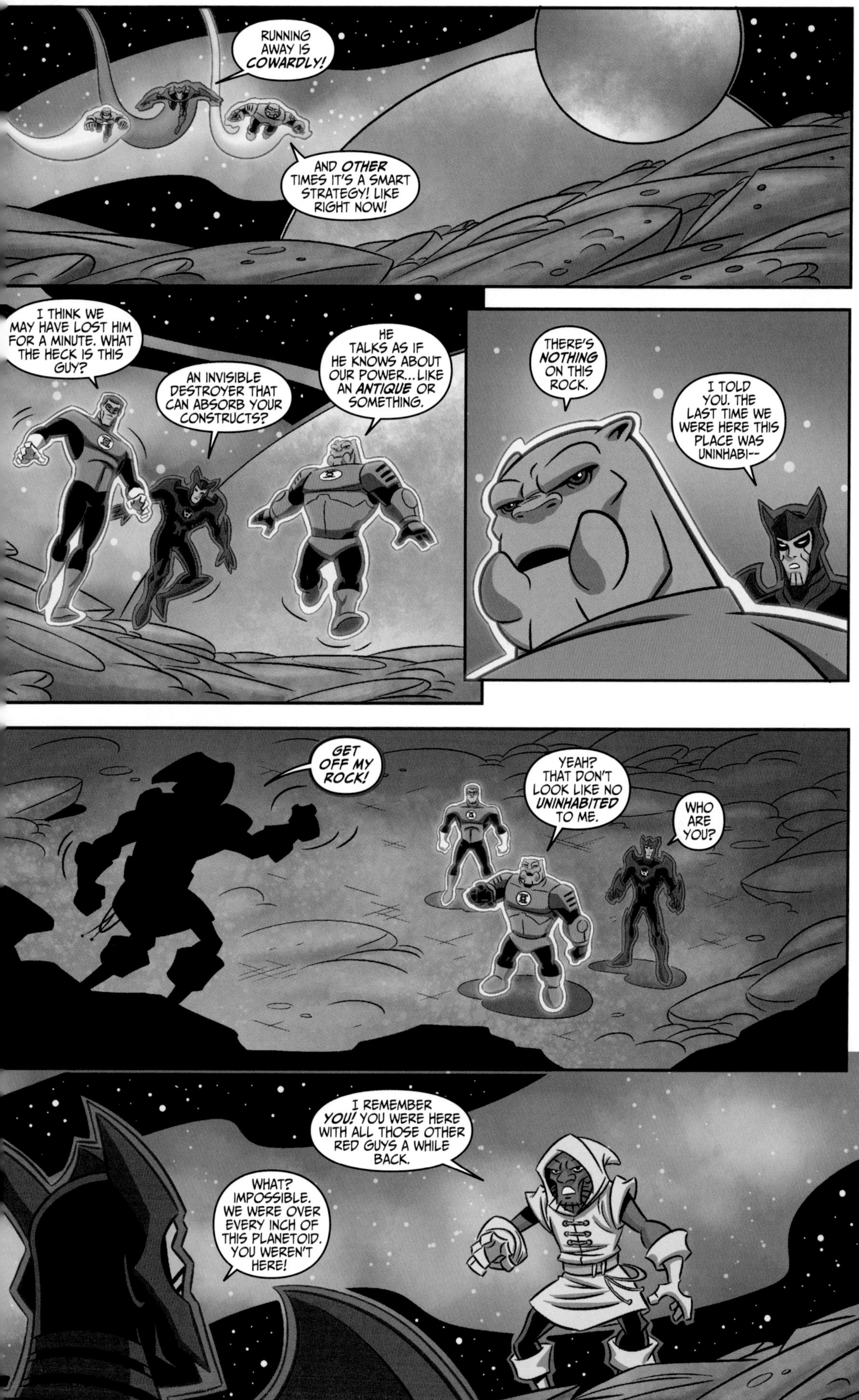
RUNNING AWAY IS COWARDLY!
AND OTHER TIMES IT'S A SMART STRATEGY! LIKE RIGHT NOW!
I THINK WE MAY HAVE LOST HIM FOR A MINUTE. WHAT THE HECK IS THIS GUY?
AN INVISIBLE DESTROYER THAT CAN ABSORB YOUR CONSTRUCTS?
HE TALKS AS IF HE KNOWS ABOUT OUR POWER...LIKE AN ANTIQUE OR SOMETHING.
THERE'S NOTHING ON THIS ROCK.
I TOLD YOU. THE LAST TIME WE WERE HERE THIS PLACE WAS UNINHABI--
GET OFF MY ROCK!
YEAH? THAT DON'T LOOK LIKE NO UNINHABITED TO ME.
WHO ARE YOU?
I REMEMBER YOU! YOU WERE HERE WITH ALL THOSE OTHER RED GUYS A WHILE BACK.
WHAT? IMPOSSIBLE. WE WERE OVER EVERY INCH OF THIS PLANETOID. YOU WEREN'T HERE!

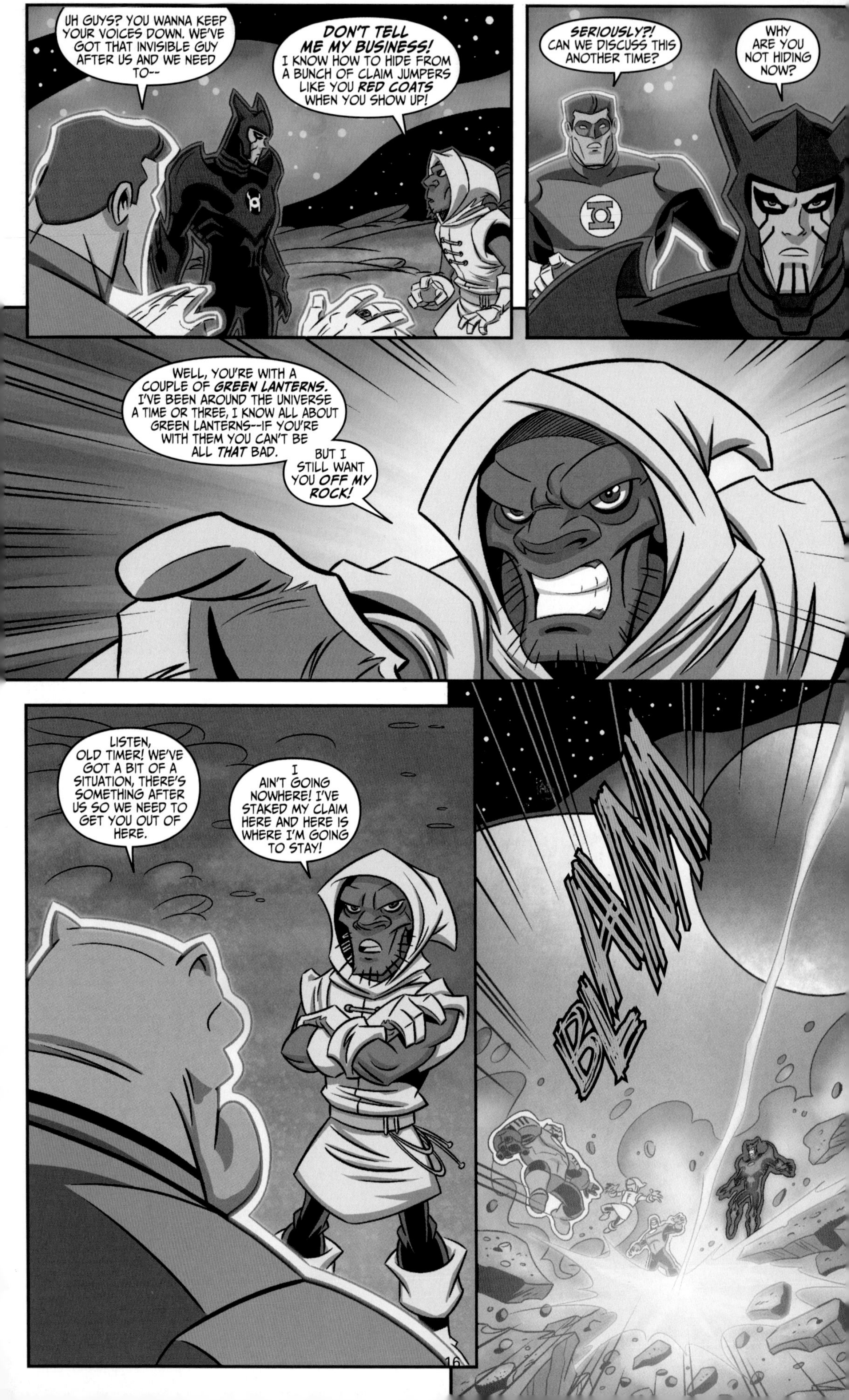
UH GUYS? YOU WANNA KEEP YOUR VOICES DOWN. WE'VE GOT THAT INVISIBLE GUY AFTER US AND WE NEED TO--
DON'T TELL ME MY BUSINESS! I KNOW HOW TO HIDE FROM A BUNCH OF CLAIM JUMPERS LIKE YOU RED COATS WHEN YOU SHOW UP!
SERIOUSLY?! CAN WE DISCUSS THIS ANOTHER TIME?
WHY ARE YOU NOT HIDING NOW?
WELL, YOU'RE WITH A COUPLE OF GREEN LANTERNS. I'VE BEEN AROUND THE UNIVERSE A TIME OR THREE, I KNOW ALL ABOUT GREEN LANTERNS--IF YOU'RE WITH THEM YOU CAN'T BE ALL THAT BAD.
BUT I STILL WANT YOU OFF MY ROCK!
LISTEN, OLD TIMER! WE'VE GOT A BIT OF A SITUATION, THERE'S SOMETHING AFTER US SO WE NEED TO GET YOU OUT OF HERE.
I AIN'T GOING NOWHERE! I'VE STAKED MY CLAIM HERE AND HERE IS WHERE I'M GOING TO STAY!
BLAM

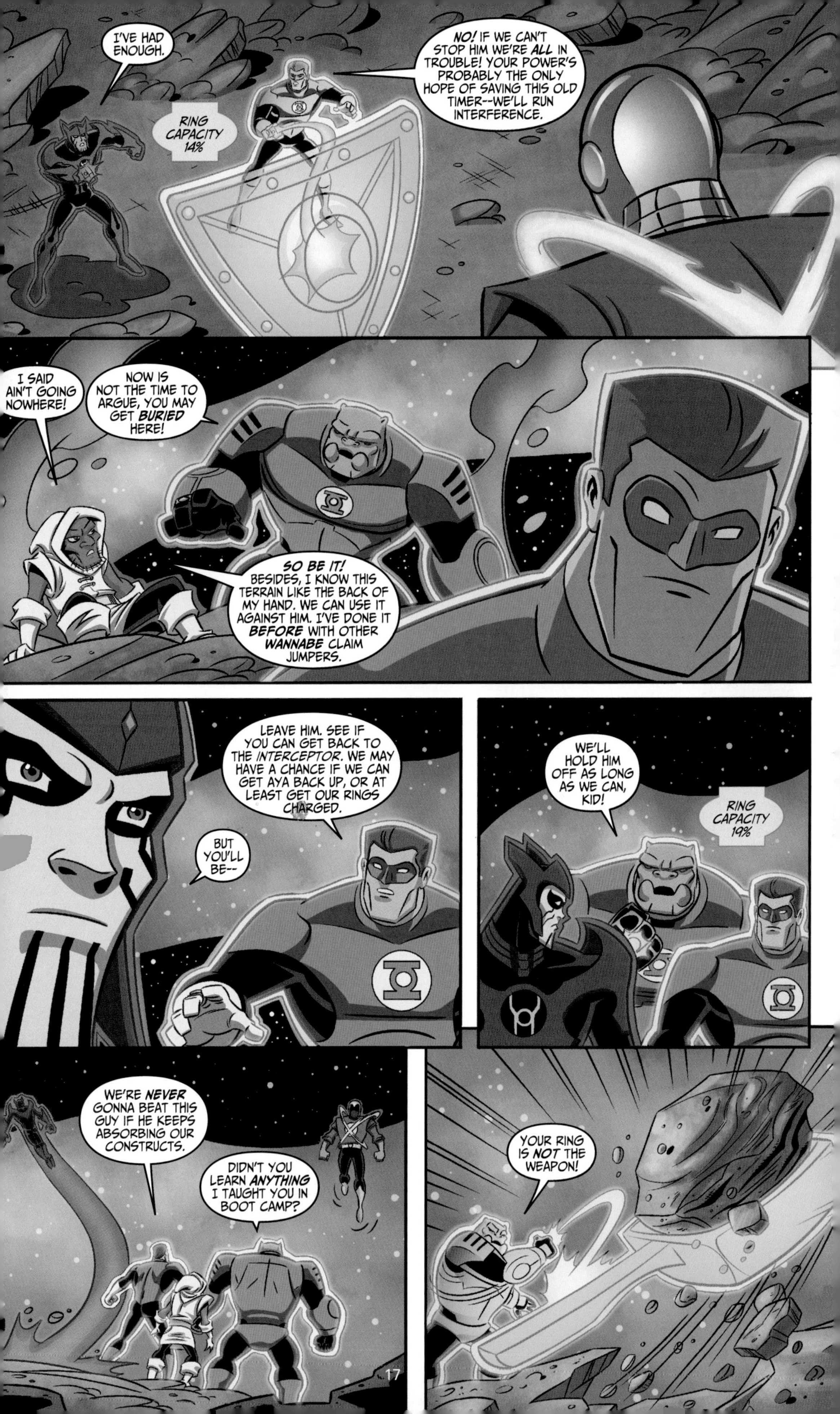

I'VE HAD ENOUGH.
RING CAPACITY 14%
NO! IF WE CAN'T STOP HIM WE'RE ALL IN TROUBLE! YOUR POWER'S PROBABLY THE ONLY HOPE OF SAVING THIS OLD TIMER--WE'LL RUN INTERFERENCE.
I SAID AIN'T GOING NOWHERE!
NOW IS NOT THE TIME TO ARGUE, YOU MAY GET BURIED HERE!
SO BE IT! BESIDES, I KNOW THIS TERRAIN LIKE THE BACK OF MY HAND. WE CAN USE IT AGAINST HIM. I'VE DONE IT BEFORE WITH OTHER WANNABE CLAIM JUMPERS.
LEAVE HIM. SEE IF YOU CAN GET BACK TO THE INTERCEPTOR. WE MAY HAVE A CHANCE IF WE CAN GET AYA BACK UP, OR AT LEAST GET OUR RINGS CHARGED.
BUT YOU'LL BE--
WE'LL HOLD HIM OFF AS LONG AS WE CAN, KID!
RING CAPACITY 19%
WE'RE NEVER GONNA BEAT THIS GUY IF HE KEEPS ABSORBING OUR CONSTRUCTS.
DIDN'T YOU LEARN ANYTHING I TAUGHT YOU IN BOOT CAMP?
YOUR RING IS NOT THE WEAPON!

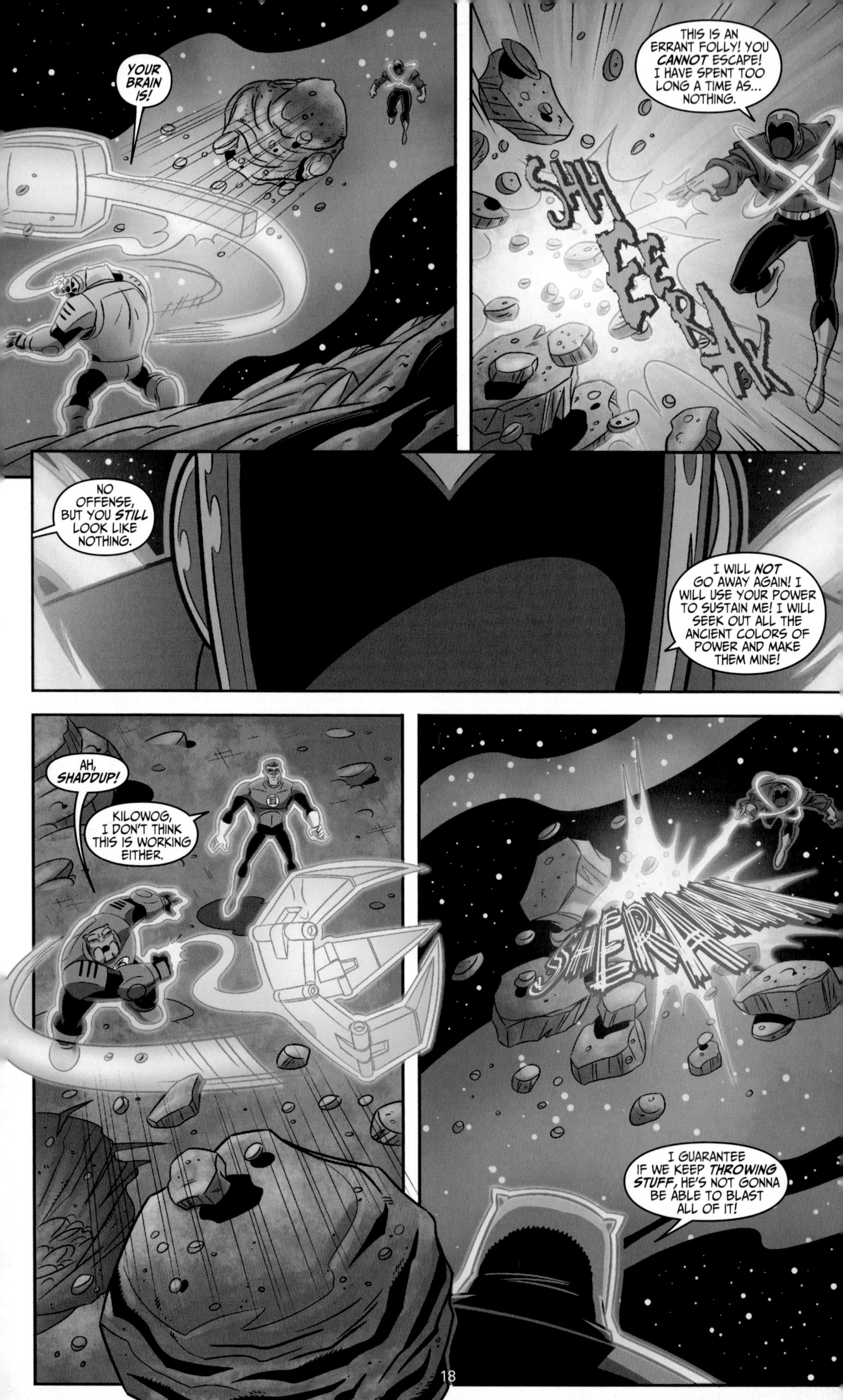
YOUR BRAIN IS!
THIS IS AN ERRANT FOLLY! YOU CANNOT ESCAPE! I HAVE SPENT TOO LONG A TIME AS... NOTHING.
SHHCCERRAK
NO OFFENSE, BUT YOU STILL LOOK LIKE NOTHING.
I WILL NOT GO AWAY AGAIN! I WILL USE YOUR POWER TO SUSTAIN ME! I WILL SEEK OUT ALL THE ANCIENT COLORS OF POWER AND MAKE THEM MINE!
AH, SHADDUP!
KILOWOG, I DON'T THINK THIS IS WORKING EITHER.
SHERAAK
I GUARANTEE IF WE KEEP THROWING STUFF, HE'S NOT GONNA BE ABLE TO BLAST ALL OF IT!

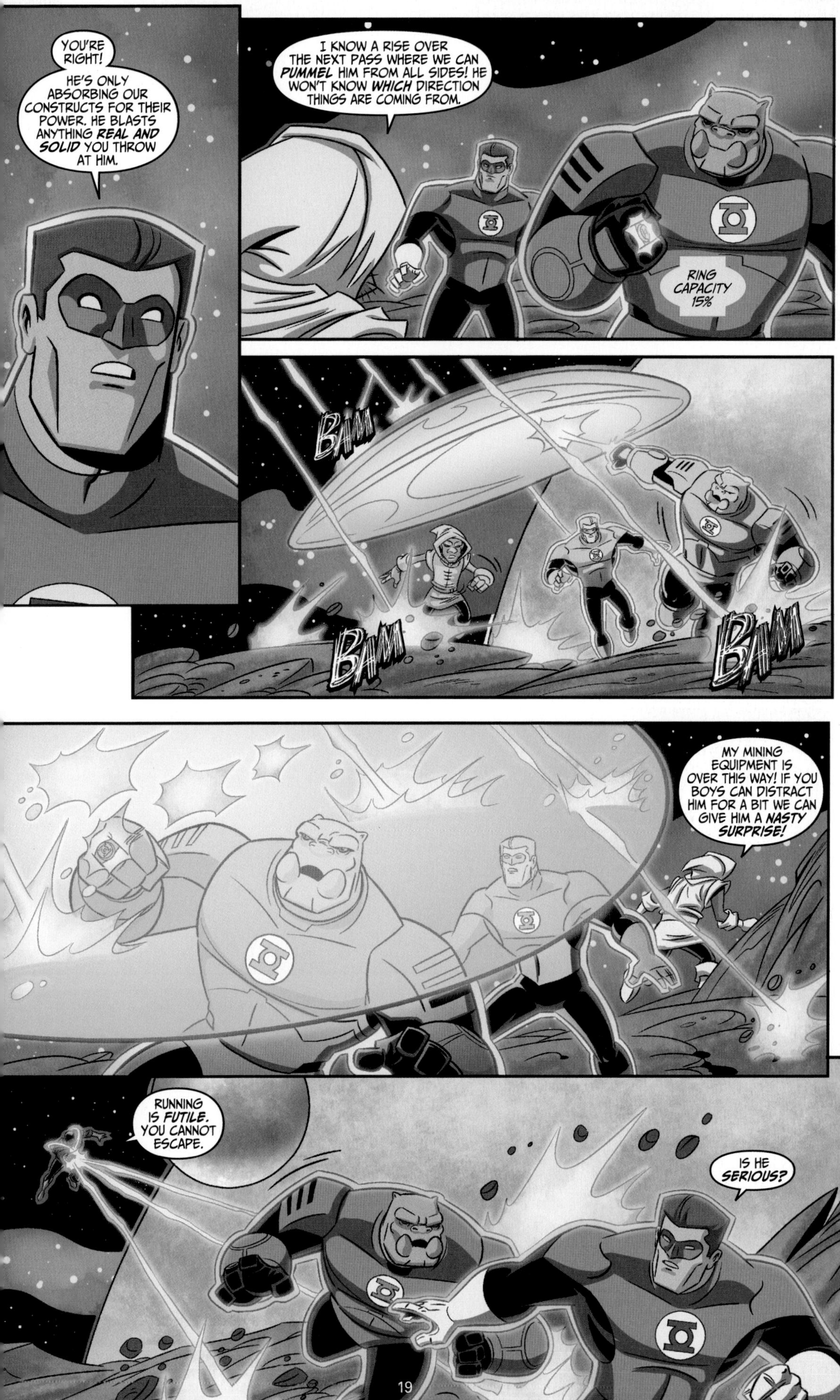
YOU'RE RIGHT!
HE'S ONLY ABSORBING OUR CONSTRUCTS FOR THEIR POWER. HE BLASTS ANYTHING REAL AND SOLID YOU THROW AT HIM.
I KNOW A RISE OVER THE NEXT PASS WHERE WE CAN PUMMEL HIM FROM ALL SIDES! HE WON'T KNOW WHICH DIRECTION THINGS ARE COMING FROM.
RING CAPACITY 15%
BAM
BAM
BAM
MY MINING EQUIPMENT IS OVER THIS WAY! IF YOU BOYS CAN DISTRACT HIM FOR A BIT WE CAN GIVE HIM A NASTY SURPRISE!
RUNNING IS FUTILE. YOU CANNOT ESCAPE.
IS HE SERIOUS?

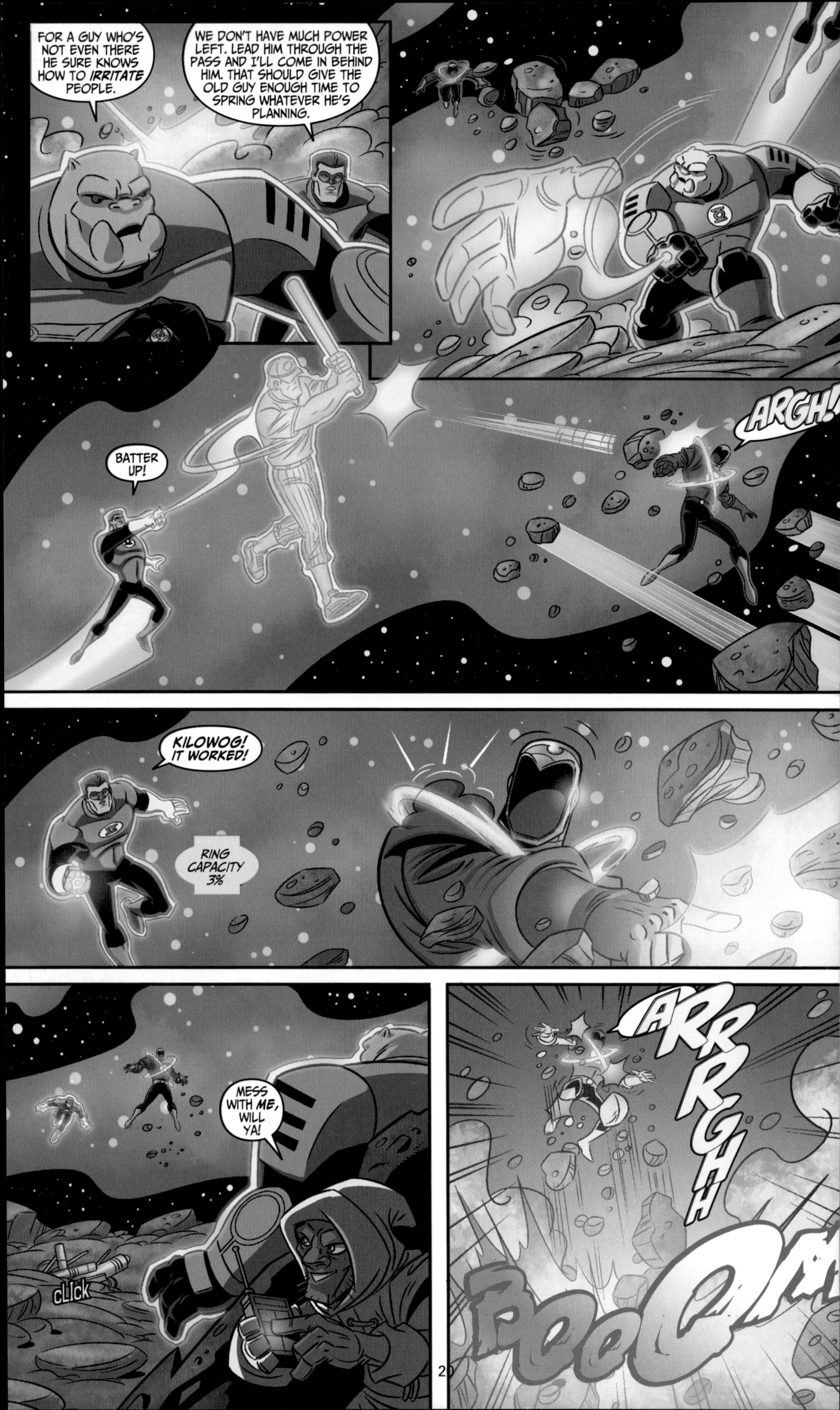

FOR A GUY WHO'S NOT EVEN THERE HE SURE KNOWS HOW TO IRRITATE PEOPLE.
WE DON'T HAVE MUCH POWER LEFT. LEAD HIM THROUGH THE PASS AND I'LL COME IN BEHIND HIM. THAT SHOULD GIVE THE OLD GUY ENOUGH TIME TO SPRING WHATEVER HE'S PLANNING.
BATTER UP!
ARGH!
KILOWOG! IT WORKED!
RING CAPACITY 3%
MESS WITH ME, WILL YA!
CLICK
ARRRGHH

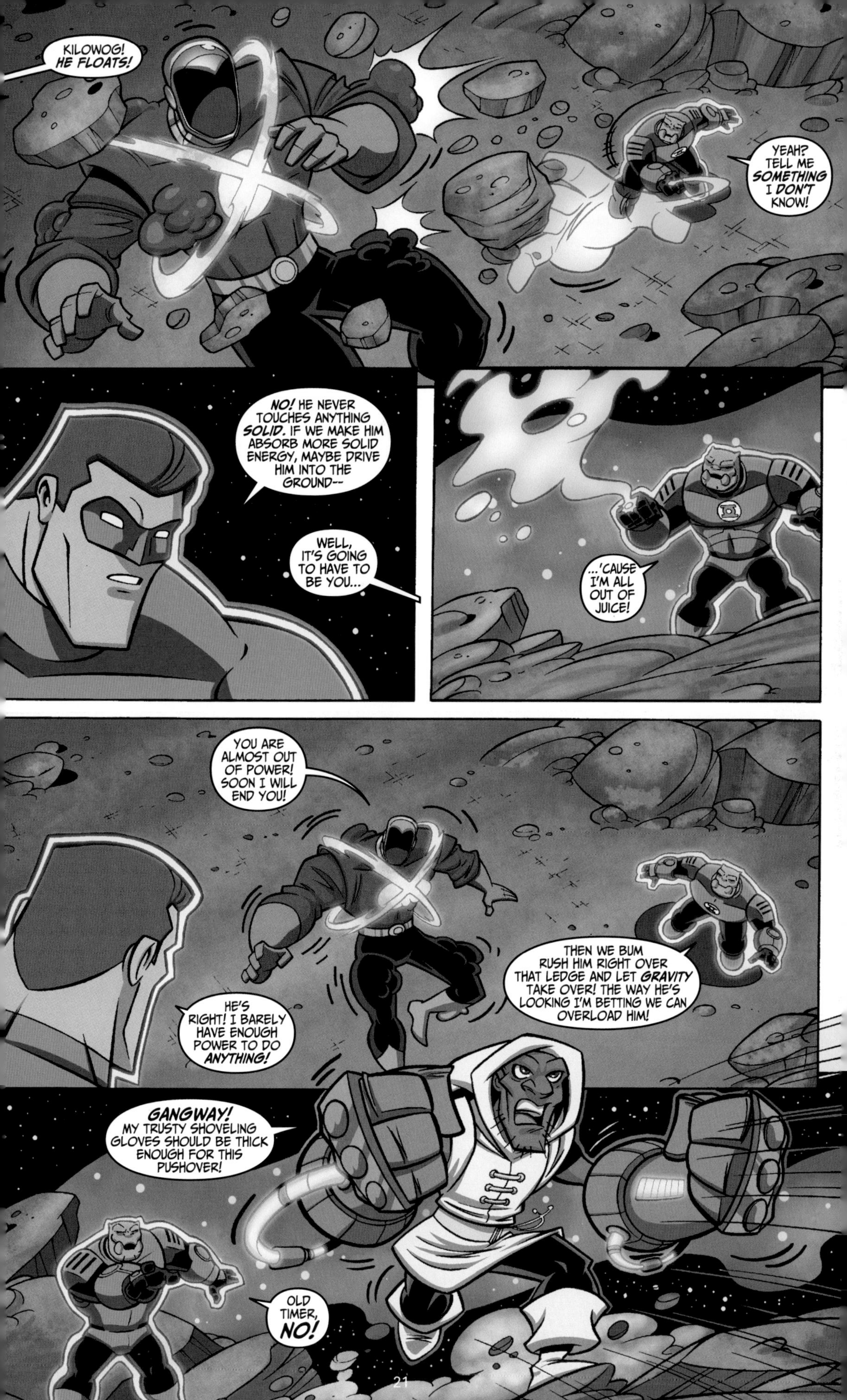
KILOWOG! HE FLOATS!
YEAH? TELL ME SOMETHING I DON'T KNOW!
NO! HE NEVER TOUCHES ANYTHING SOLID. IF WE MAKE HIM ABSORB MORE SOLID ENERGY, MAYBE DRIVE HIM INTO THE GROUND--
WELL, IT'S GOING TO HAVE TO BE YOU...
...'CAUSE I'M ALL OUT OF JUICE!
YOU ARE ALMOST OUT OF POWER! SOON I WILL END YOU!
HE'S RIGHT! I BARELY HAVE ENOUGH POWER TO DO ANYTHING!
THEN WE BUM RUSH HIM RIGHT OVER THAT LEDGE AND LET GRAVITY TAKE OVER! THE WAY HE'S LOOKING I'M BETTING WE CAN OVERLOAD HIM!
GANGWAY! MY TRUSTY SHOVELING GLOVES SHOULD BE THICK ENOUGH FOR THIS PUSHOVER!
OLD TIMER, NO!

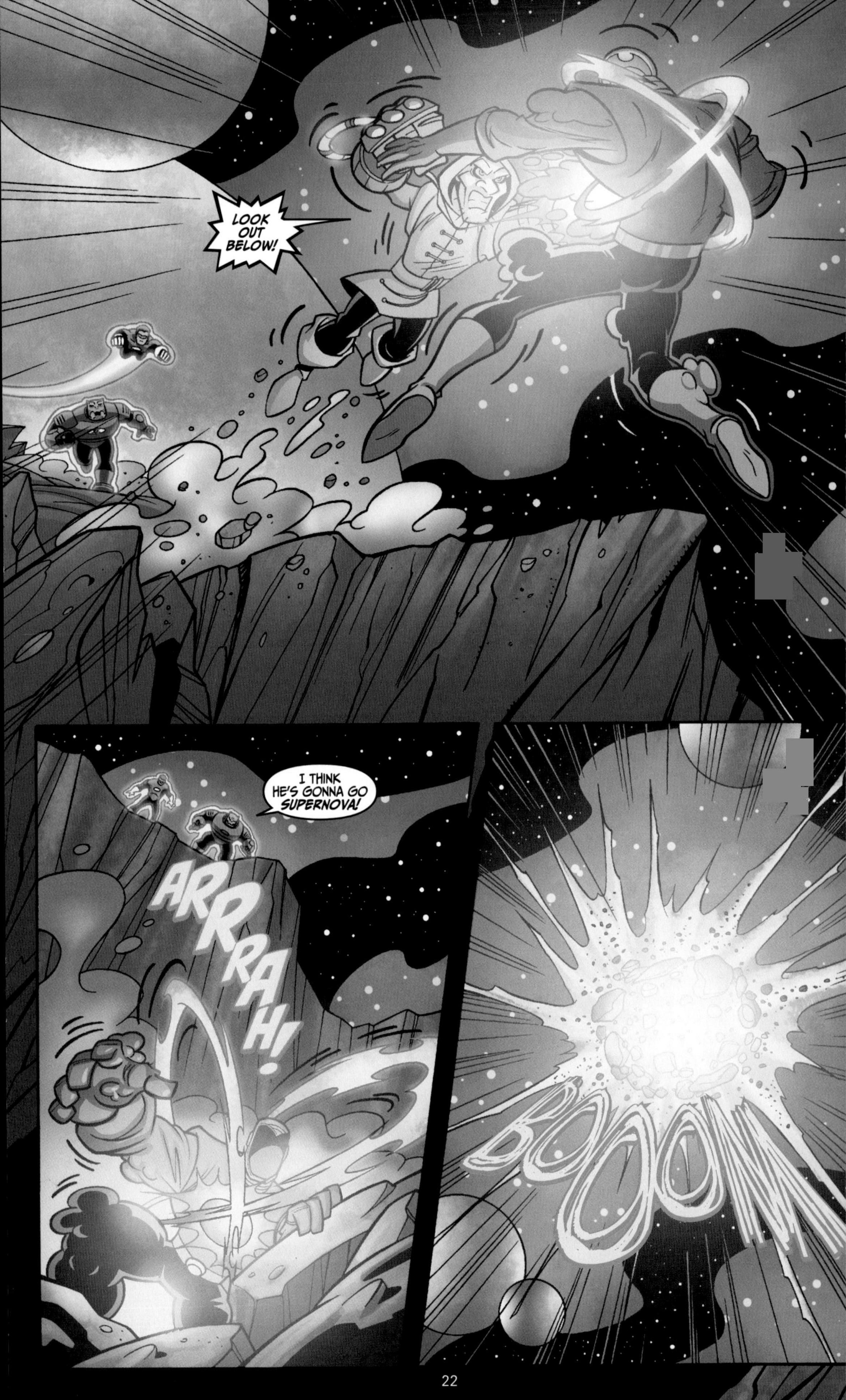
LOOK OUT BELOW!
I THINK HE'S GONNA GO SUPERNOVA!
ARRRAH!
BOOOOM

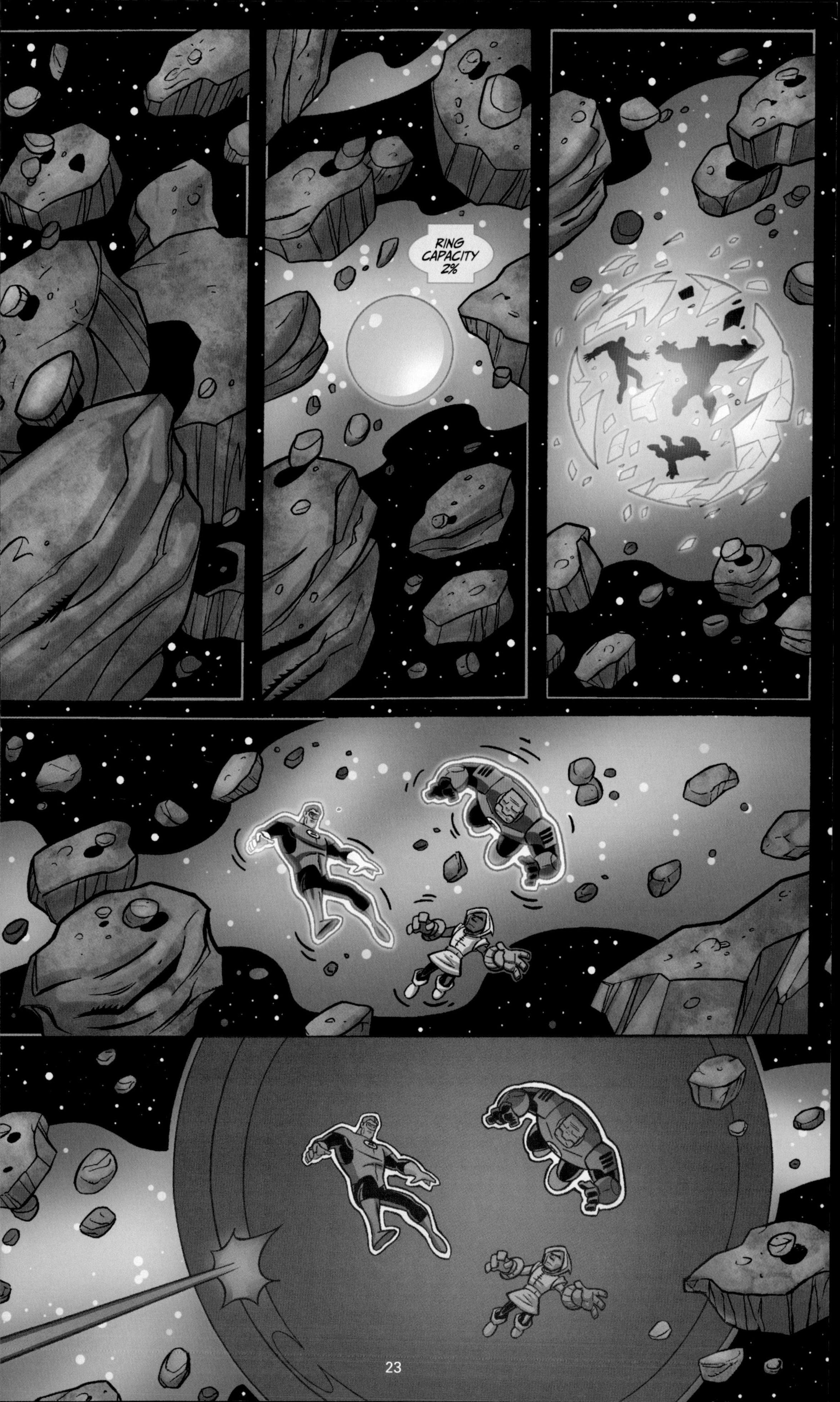
RING CAPACITY 2%

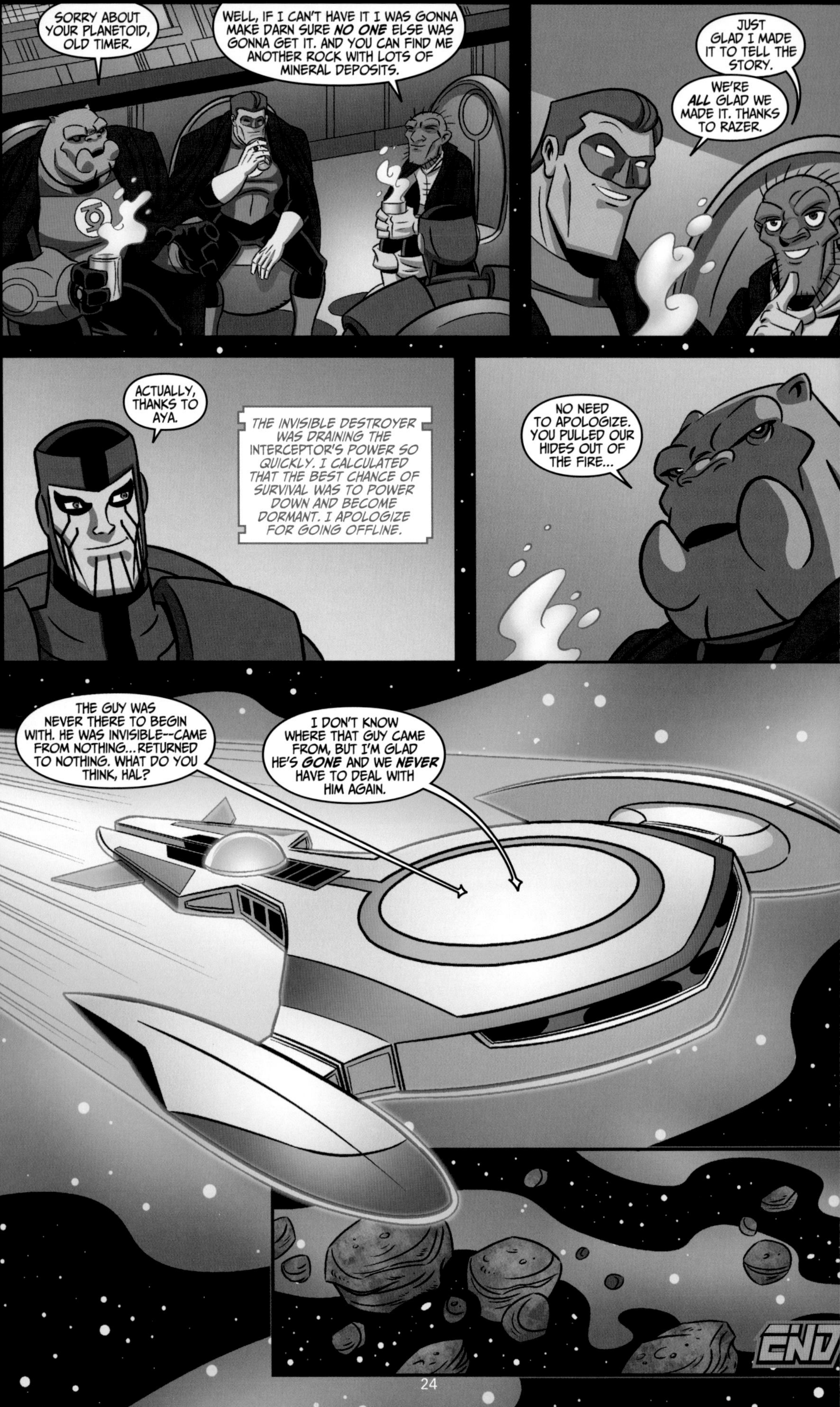
SORRY ABOUT YOUR PLANETOID, OLD TIMER.
WELL, IF I CAN'T HAVE IT I WAS GONNA MAKE DARN SURE NO ONE ELSE WAS GONNA GET IT. AND YOU CAN FIND ME ANOTHER ROCK WITH LOTS OF MINERAL DEPOSITS.
JUST GLAD I MADE IT TO TELL THE STORY.
WE'RE ALL GLAD WE MADE IT. THANKS TO RAZER.
ACTUALLY, THANKS TO AYA.
THE INVISIBLE DESTROYER WAS DRAINING THE INTERCEPTOR'S POWER SO QUICKLY. I CALCULATED THAT THE BEST CHANCE OF SURVIVAL WAS TO POWER DOWN AND BECOME DORMANT. I APOLOGIZE FOR GOING OFFLINE.
NO NEED TO APOLOGIZE. YOU PULLED OUR HIDES OUT OF THE FIRE...
THE GUY WAS NEVER THERE TO BEGIN WITH. HE WAS INVISIBLE--CAME FROM NOTHING...RETURNED TO NOTHING. WHAT DO YOU THINK, HAL?
I DON'T KNOW WHERE THAT GUY CAME FROM, BUT I'M GLAD HE'S GONE AND WE NEVER HAVE TO DEAL WITH HIM AGAIN.
END

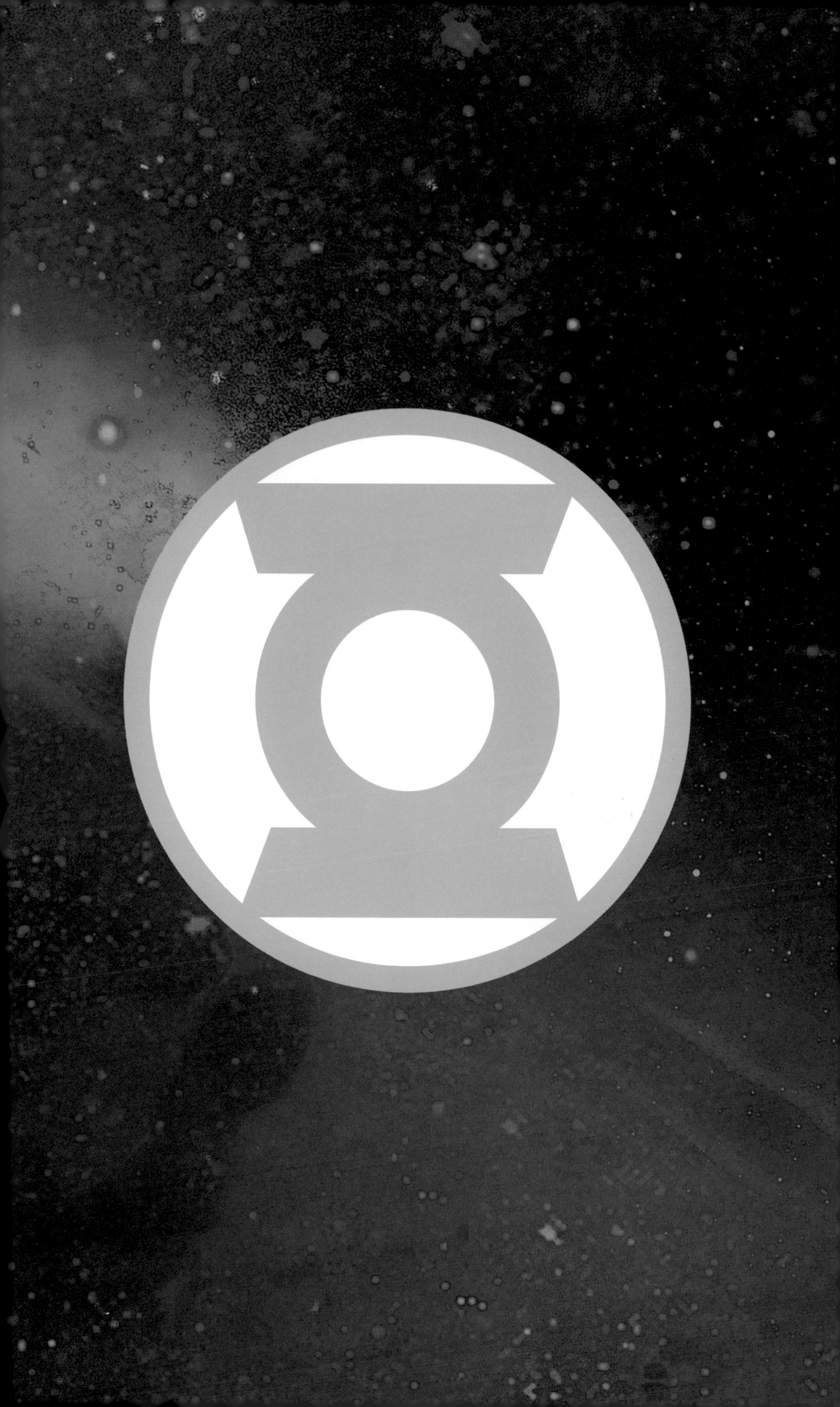

DRAW YOUR OWN GREEN LANTERN
KILOWOG!

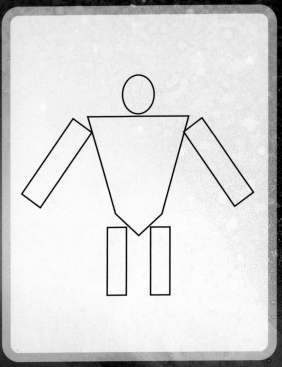

1.) Using a pencil, start with some basic shapes to build a "body."

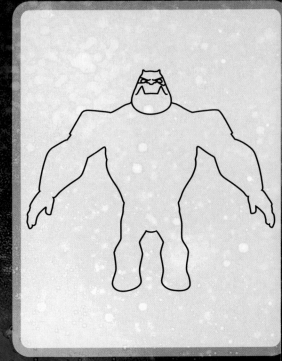

2.) Smooth your outline, and begin adding facial features.

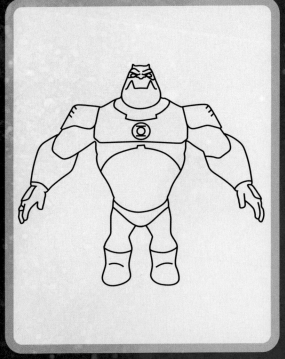

3.) Add in costume details, like Kilowog's suit, gloves, and Green Lantern symbol.

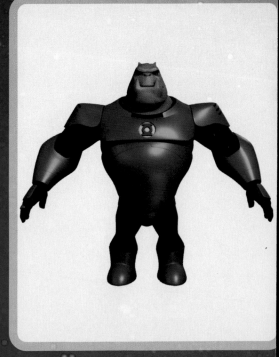

4.) Fill in the colors with crayons or markers.

CREATORS

ART BALTAZAR *writer*

Art Baltazar is a cartoonist machine from the heart of Chicago! He defines cartoons and comics not only as an art style, but as a way of life. Currently, Art is the creative force behind *The New York Times* best-selling, Eisner Award-winning, DC Comics series Tiny Titans, and the co-writer for *Billy Batson and the Magic of SHAZAM!* and co-creator of the Superman Family Adventures series. Art is living the dream! He draws comics and never has to leave the house. He lives with his lovely wife, Rose, big boy Sonny, little boy Gordon, and little girl Audrey. Right on!

FRANCO AURELIANI *writer*

Bronx, New York born writer and artist Franco Aureliani has been drawing comics since he could hold a crayon. Currently residing in upstate New York with his wife, Ivette, and son, Nicolas, Franco spends most of his days in a Batcave-like studio where he produces DC's Tiny Titans comics. In 1995, Franco founded Blindwolf Studios, an independent art studio where he and fellow creators can create children's comics. Franco is the creator, artist, and writer of *Weirdsville, L'il Creeps,* and *Eagle All Star,* as well as the co-creator and writer of *Patrick the Wolf Boy.* When he's not writing and drawing, Franco also teaches high school art.

DARIO BRIZUELA *illustrator*

Dario Brizuela is a professional comic book artist. He's illustrated some of today's most popular characters, including Batman, Green Lantern, Teenage Mutant Ninja Turtles, Thor, Iron Man, and Transformers. His best-known works for DC Comics include the series DC Super Friends, Justice League Unlimited, and Batman: The Brave and the Bold.

GLOSSARY

asteroid (ASS-tuh-roid) — a small, rocky planetoid that travels around the sun

desolate (DESS-uh-luht) — deserted or uninhabited

futile (FYOO-tuhl) — useless and a waste of time

galaxy (GAL-uhk-see) — a very large group of stars and planets

gravity (GRAV-uh-tee) — the force that pulls things down toward the surface of Earth

planetoid (PLAN-ih-toyd) — a small, celestial body resembling a planet, such as an asteroid

rage (RAYJ) — very strong and uncontrolled anger

supernova (soo-pur-NOH-vuh) — an exploding star that can give off millions of times more light than the sun

willpower (WIL-pou-ur) — strong determination

VISUAL QUESTIONS

1. On pages 17–18, Kilowog tells Hal Jordan, "Your ring is not the weapon. Your brain is!" What do you think Kilowog means by this statement?

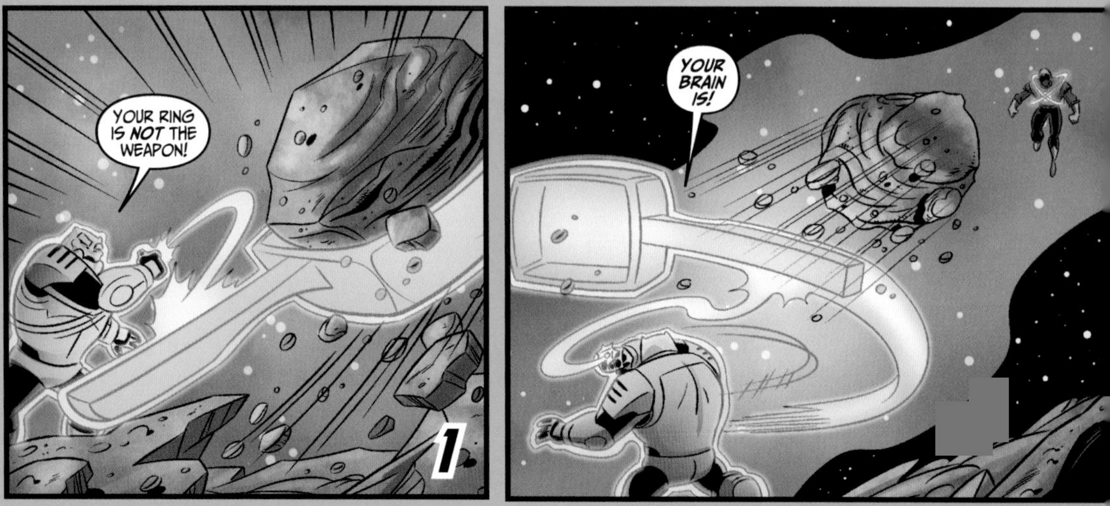
YOUR RING IS NOT THE WEAPON!
1
YOUR BRAIN IS!

2. With his powerful green ring, Hal Jordan can create anything he imagines. If you wore a power ring, what would you create? Why?

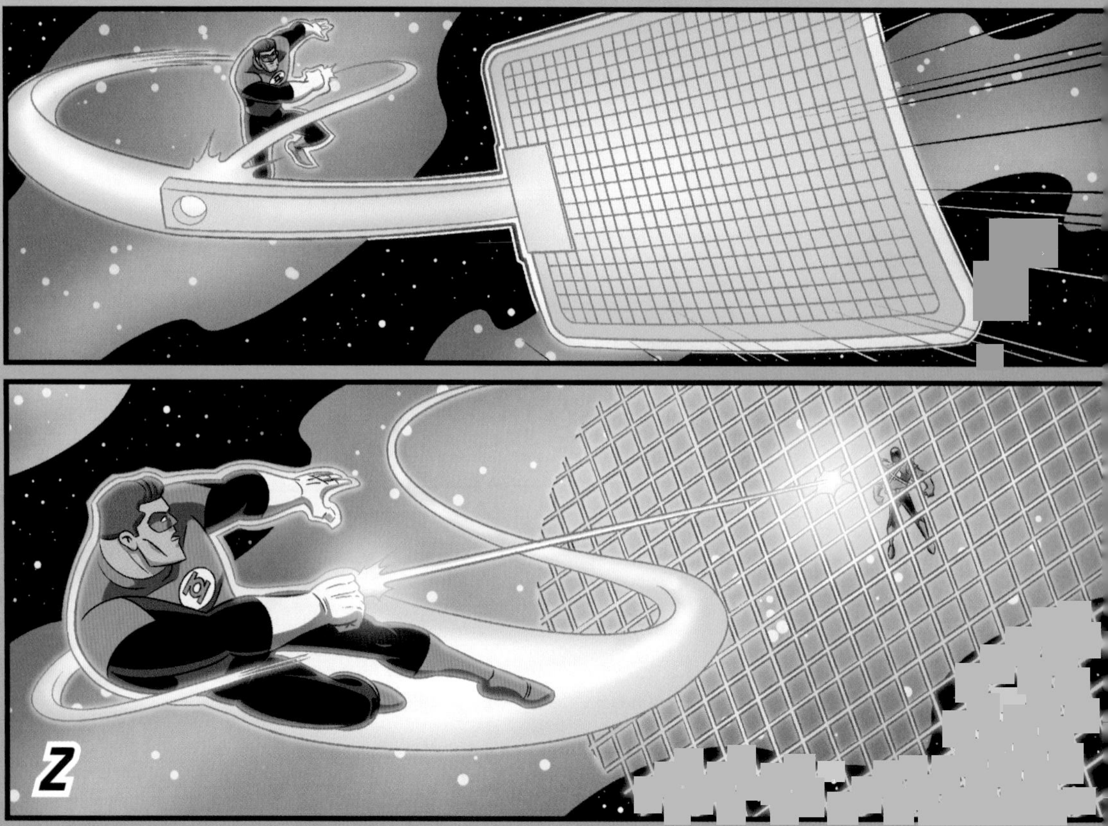
2

3. **Hal Jordan, Kilowog, Razer, Aya, and even the Old Timer worked together to defeat the Invisible Destroyer. Who do you think played the most important role in this mission, and why?**

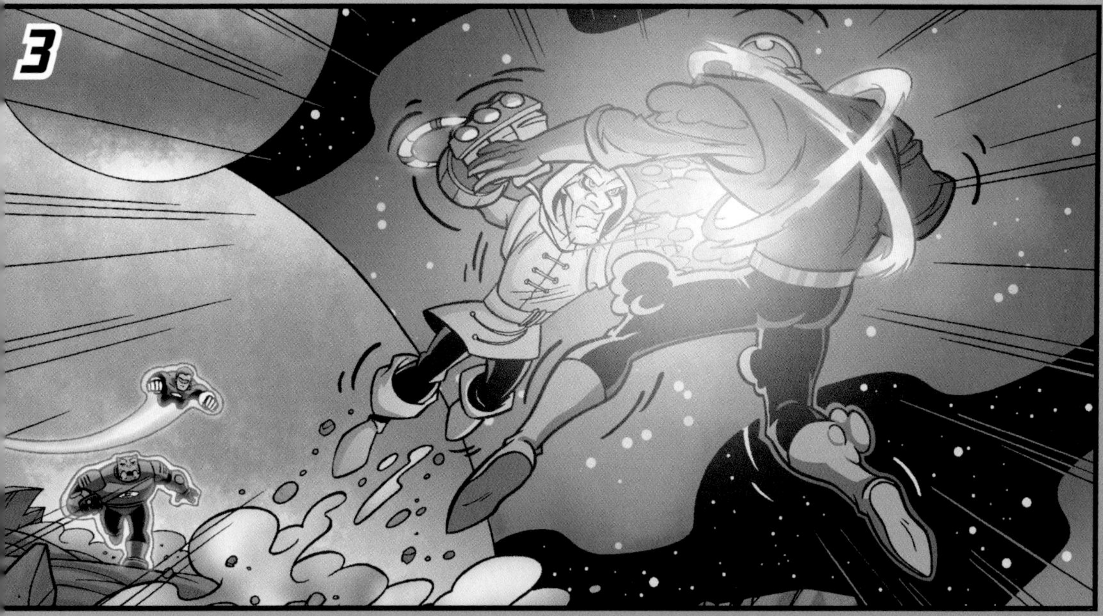
3

4. **In comic books, action often happens in the space between panels. Study the two panels below from page 23. Then describe what is happening between the panels. What clues helped you follow the story from one panel to the next?**

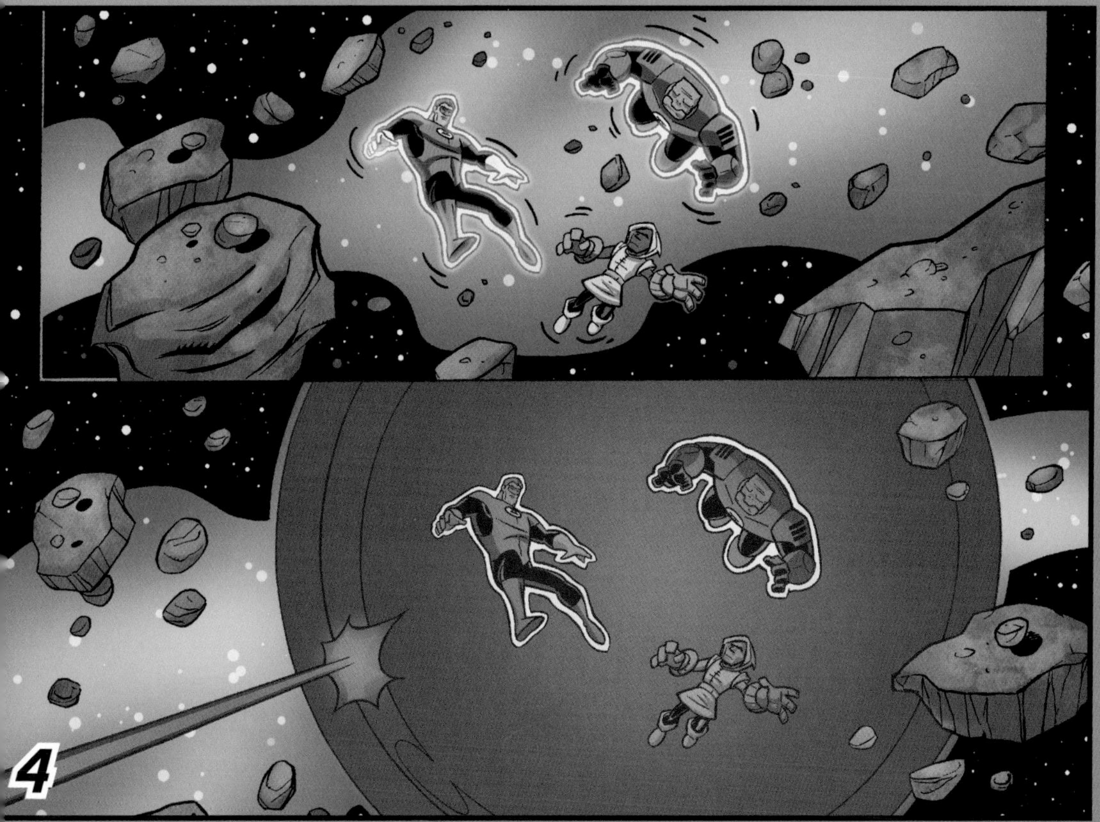
4

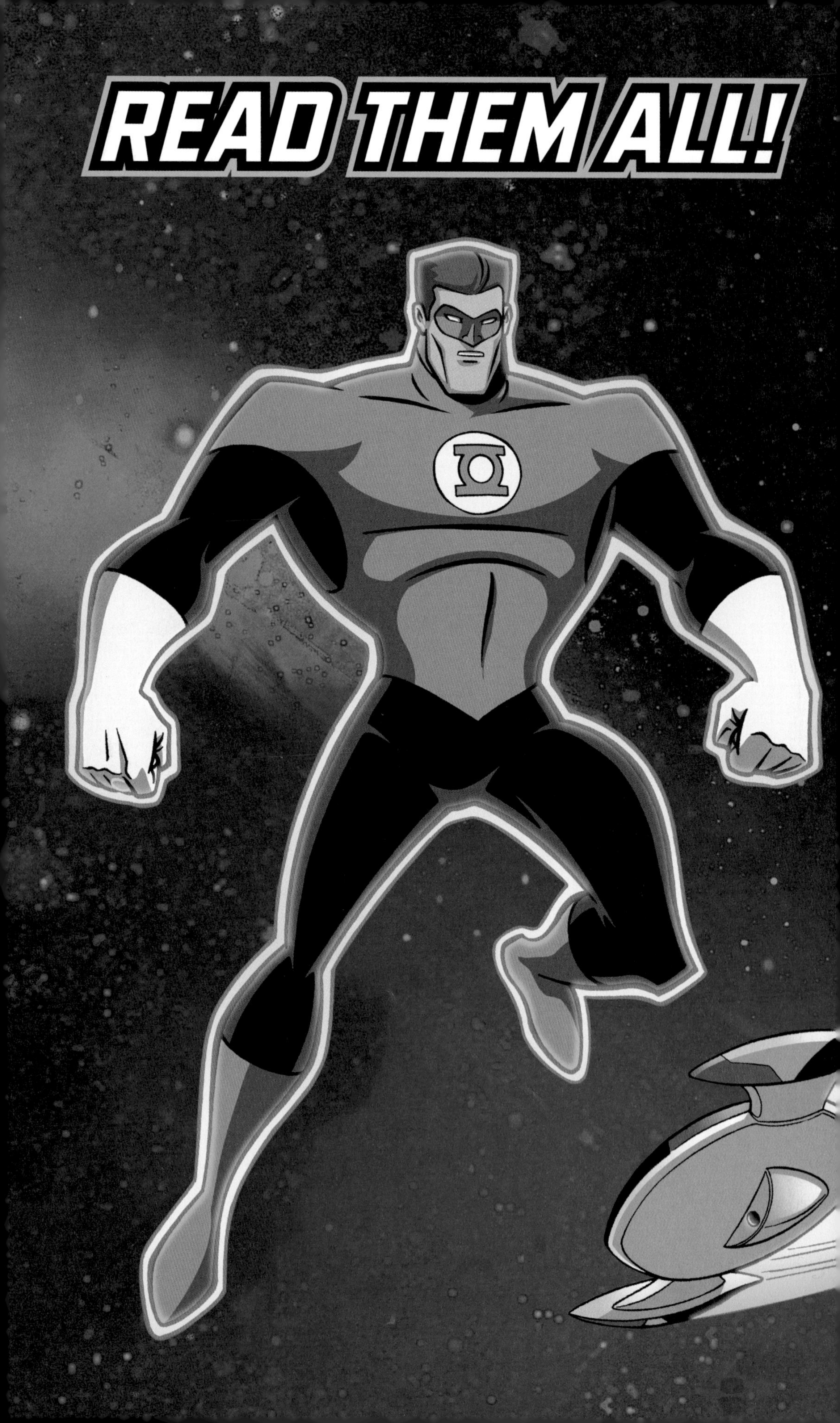
READ THEM ALL!

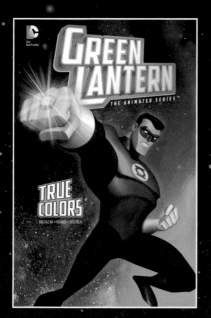

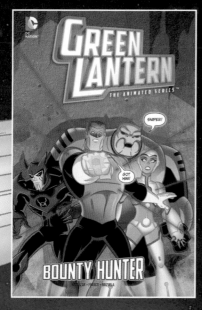

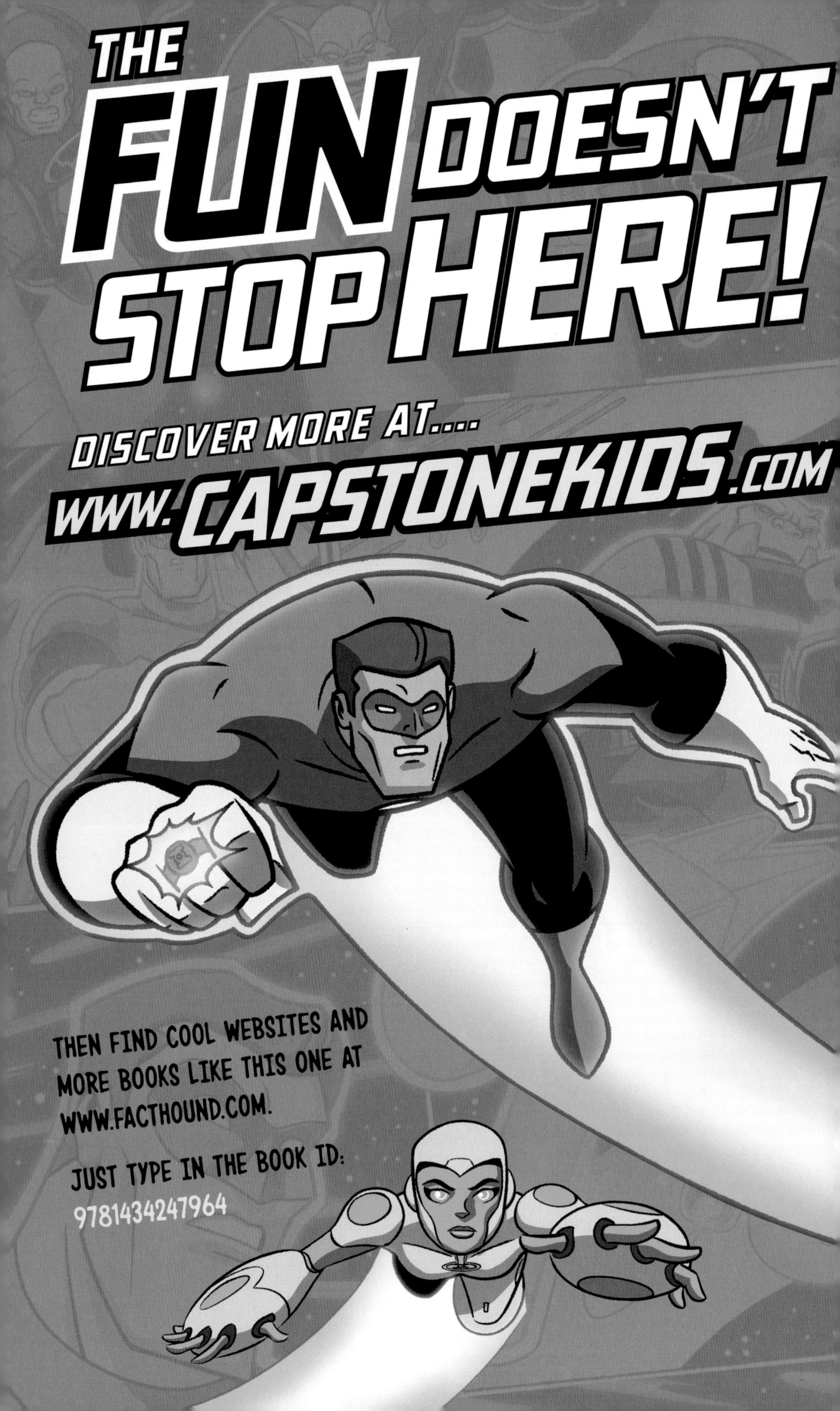
THE FUN DOESN'T STOP HERE!
DISCOVER MORE AT....
WWW.CAPSTONEKIDS.COM
THEN FIND COOL WEBSITES AND MORE BOOKS LIKE THIS ONE AT WWW.FACTHOUND.COM.
JUST TYPE IN THE BOOK ID:
9781434247964